To Dance with Destiny

By

Lillian Delaney

ISBN: 1-4033-5186-4 (e-book)
ISBN: 1-4033-5187-2 (Paperback)
ISBN: 1-4033-5188-0 (Hardcover)

This book is printed on acid free paper.

1stBooks - rev. 08/16/02

Table of Content

Chapter 1

The hot and humid April wind stirred the dry leaves on the trees. Even at 8:00 o'clock in the morning, the air was stifling. Ruth knew from experience that the day would rapidly turn into a real scorcher.

She gathered her papers and books into her arms and hurried quickly from the small parking lot to the front door of the old church. She fumbled with her keys almost dropping her books, and finally managed to unlock the door. It swung open easily and the morning sun flooded the small room with its bright light.

Ruth gave the door a shove with one foot before she hurried to the piano bench and dropped her books. With her arms now free, she began to thumb through the stack of papers and pulled out a sheet of music. She studied it for a moment while she hummed a tune softly to herself.

The melody and her thoughts carried her back to another time…a time, which seemed like only yesterday. How quickly the years disappeared. Lost in her thoughts, Ruth didn't hear the door open until the sound of someone clearing their throat startled her.

Ruth jumped at the sound, which echoed loudly in the empty room. She jerked around to face the man standing by the door. Her heart was pounding but her voice was steady.

"Oh! You startled me! I didn't hear you come in. Can I help you?" Ruth could see at a glance that this man was not one of the many poor and hungry that normally came to the Church for food.

"I would like to see Reverend Bystander."

1

Lillian Delaney

"He hasn't arrived just yet." Ruth glanced at her watch and scolded herself for her remark. Jacob had warned her many times never to admit she was alone. *'Always say I am unavailable. Don't say I am not here.'* "He should be arriving anytime if you would like to wait?"

The man started backing toward the door; he held a hat in his hands and began to turn it around and around as he spoke. "I'll come back."

Before Ruth could ask his name, the man had backed out the door and was gone. She quickly crossed the floor and looked out the door. There was no sign of the man. He had disappeared. Something in his behavior was odd. She could not put her finger on just what it was, but a gnawing sense of—what was it…panic, fear, foreboding…or maybe it was just that she was still shaken at having been startled—something gripped her stomach.

Ruth slowly closed the door and went back to her music. She found her selection again and sat at the piano. She played the notes absent mindedly as the melody transported her back in time. With her eyes closed and the hint of a smile playing with the corner of her mouth, Ruth began to sing softly.

"When doubt and disappointment hide the morning sun, when all my dreams are ended, all my songs are sung. His spirit soars within me, every doubt is gone, I see a new horizon and sing a brand new song…"

"It's a beautiful song." The words were soft and tender, and very close behind her.

"Jacob!" Ruth took a playful swing at her husband as he dodged the blow and quickly wrapped her in his arms in a warm embrace.

Jacob laughed and gave Ruth a quick kiss on the neck. "I'm sorry, I just couldn't resist!"

"You're always sneaking up on me and scaring me. Twice in one day is more than I need."

"Sorry...it brings back memories doesn't it?" Jacob indicated the music on the piano with a nod of his head.

"Good memories."

"And sad." The flat statement hid a question.

"Bittersweet perhaps. Without the past...there would be no present. I would not want to change the present and we cannot change the past."

Jacob sighed and sat down on the piano bench next to his wife. "You're right of course."

"I would like to sing it tonight if you don't mind." Ruth looked at her husband with a question in her eyes. She was watching for an indication of his thoughts.

After a slight pause, Jacob answered. "I think it would be a fitting remembrance on this 30th anniversary."

Both Jacob and Ruth sat in silence for a moment, then something that Ruth had said finally registered with him. "What did you mean by *'twice in one day'*?"

"Oh, there was another man here earlier to see you. I didn't hear him come in and he startled me. That's all."

A note of irritation could be heard in Jacob's voice. "You didn't lock the door behind you again did you?"

"I had my hands full and I knew you would be here any minute." Ruth tried to look busy with her music.

"That isn't the point. You could have been hurt. *LOCK THE DOOR* when you're here alone, even if it is only for a few minutes. You forget how much things have changed." In a softer tone, "I couldn't bear to have anything happen to you."

Ruth smiled and ran her finger along the jaw line of Jacob's face. "I am very good at reading faces. He wasn't dangerous; he was just nervous."

Jacob took Ruth's hand in his. "How do you know he wasn't dangerous? Was he wearing a sign that said *'I'm not dangerous; I won't hurt you'*?"

Ruth laughed. "Don't be silly...I could tell by his eyes." Ruth leaned close to Jacob and stared into his eyes then continued with meaning in her voice. "You know how good I am at reading eyes."

Jacob wrapped his arms around his wife again and gave her a tight squeeze and a kiss before letting her go. "Lock the door!"

"Okay! Okay! I'll lock the door."

"Now, what did he say?"

"Nothing really...he wouldn't talk to me. He wanted to see you, and he wouldn't wait. He said he would be back later."

Jacob looked at his watch. "I guess he'll return if it's important. It's getting late, I better get to work." He gave his wife another quick kiss and started to rise, but movement in the direction of the door caught his eye.

Jacob stood to his feet and addressed the man standing by the door. "Hello. Can I help you?"

"Reverend Bystander," the man took a couple of steps forward, "do you remember me?"

Jacob studied the face of the man. He was clean-shaven and looked to be about fifty-five years of age. Jacob hesitated. "I'm not...sure...something seems familiar, but I'm not sure what." It was true. Something in the eyes and the voice sparked a vague memory. The same spark made Jacob's stomach tighten. "What is your name?"

"Carlos Santine." He waited to see the Reverend Bystander's reaction to his name before he continued. "I would like to visit with you for a few minutes. It is very important. Can we speak privately?"

"We can talk in my office." Jacob indicated one of two doors on the other side of the room.

"That will work."

Both men made their way into the small office. Jacob walked around the desk and waited for Carlos to sit before continuing. "Now, what can I do for you today Mr. Santine?"

"You still don't quite remember me do you?" He did not wait for a response. "I was once acquainted with a fun loving group of guys called the 'Wily Bunch'...of course that was thirty years ago...do you remember them?"

When Jacob did not respond, Carlos continued.

"I often had, what you might call, 'business dealings' with them. I especially remember two members of the group named Jacob and Jonas." Carlos was becoming more confident. He could see that his words were achieving the desired effect.

Jacob watched as Carlos pulled a pocket watch from his jeans. He opened and closed it several times, held it up and studied it, and then finally laid it on the desk in front of him. Jacob's eyes had been fastened on the watch throughout this ritual but now returned to the man who set across the desk. "They were very interesting brothers, Jacob and Jonas, very sad, too. One of them was arrested then killed trying to escape from jail. The other one...went on with his life."

Jacob sat quietly and listened while the tightness in his stomach grew. His eyes were drawn to the watch on the

desk. He tried not to look at it but couldn't seem to stop.
Finally, he decided it was pointless to try. It was obvious
that Carlos wanted him to look at it.

"May I see the watch?" Jacob took it in his hand without
waiting for an answer.

"My brother-in-law died a month ago and I found it
among his possessions. Curious thing about my brother-in-
law, he worked as a guard at the jail in Brownsville. Didn't
make much money, but he was always "finding" things just
lying around. I wouldn't be surprised if that watch once
belonged to one of the prisoners at the jail.

Jacob's eyes never moved from the gold object he held
in his hand. He pressed the button that opened the cover as
the chain dangled between his fingers.

Carlos continued. "In fact, I seem to remember seeing a
watch just like that one. It belonged to one of those
brothers I mentioned. But I get a little confused. My
memory, perhaps, is not as good as it used to be."

Jacob looked up at Carlos. "This is all very fascinating
Mr. Santine, but how can I help you today?"

Carlos was beginning to smile. It was a twisted little
smile that was all too familiar to Jacob. "But don't you
want to hear the rest of my story?"

"I'm sure your story is very interesting; however, I
would rather hear why you have come here today?" Jacob
snapped the watch closed, pushed his chair back, and
walked to the window. He could see Carlos watching him
out of the corner of his eye, but he didn't care. His attention
was focused on a gravestone resting under the shade of big
mesquite tree.

"The watch raises some very interesting questions
regarding the death of Jonas Bystander don't you think? I

thought that perhaps you might want to put any unpleasant questions regarding this watch and the two brothers to rest."

Jacob did not turn around. "And how would I do that?"

"It is all very simple really. I do you a favor and you do me a favor."

"What kind of a favor?" Jacob turned to face Carlos.

"I work for some very important fellows who were not very happy with the Bystander brothers thirty years ago. But they are willing to let dead dogs lie, so to speak" Carlos chuckled at what he thought was a very funny play on words, "if you are willing to help them clean up some dirty linen that they have laying around."

"May I keep the watch?"

"Keep it; I don't need it...now."

"I will need to pray about your request and talk with my wife."

Carlos was confident that he already knew the answer. What else could it be? The very prominent Reverend Jacob Bystander had too much to lose. He dropped a piece of paper on the desk. "You can reach me at this number. Don't take too long." Carlos shrugged his shoulders. "My boss...he gets impatient." He left without saying another word. Jacob stood beside the window and again opened the watch. He read the inscription on the inside as a cloud passed over his face and a solitary tear ran down his cheek. He was still in this position when Ruth entered the room.

"Jacob?"

"Have you ever thought about how our lives are shaped by the decisions we make? We start out traveling down a certain road...then we come to a place of decision." Jacob waved his hand from left to right in a sweeping motion.

"We can go left or we can go right, and based on that decision...our entire future is determined."

Ruth knew something was terribly wrong and went to stand next to her husband. He instinctively, from years of habit, put his arm around her.

"Each path we travel, or don't travel, holds its own destiny. We can choose the destiny God has for us, or we can go another way...but *WE* make the choice."

Ruth searched his face. "Jacob, what is it?"

Jacob looked down at his wife. "Ruth, we talked about the possibility of having to face the truth someday. Someday has come. The man who came today was Carlos Santine. He knew the Bystander brothers thirty years ago. He brought this."

Ruth looked at the gold watch in her husband's hand puzzled. "A watch?"

"It belonged to my brother."

Now she understood. Yes, now she remembered. The watch he had shown her once, the one that had belonged to their father. "What did he want?"

"He...rather, his boss...wants me to 'laundry' money—drug money."

"What do you want to do?"

"There is only one thing to do. I will have to tell the truth. I cannot do what they ask, and the only way to protect what we have spent our lives building is to confess and step down. We will have to let someone else take over. It will not be an easy path." Jacob took Ruth's hands in his and searched her eyes for approval.

"We always new this day would come...in God's time. We can do it together and with God's help."

8

Jacob pulled Ruth to him and held her close, the pocket watch still dangled by its chain between his fingers. "To everything there is a season, a time for every purpose under heaven."

Ruth finished it for him. "A time to be born and a time to die. A time to plant, and a time to pluck up that which is planted."

"We've been planted a long time...it will be hard to leave this place. We've had so many good years here. There is a memory in every squeaky door, creaky board, and rattling window pane."

"Memories are more than doors, boards, and window panes, they are dreams we take with us no matter where we go."

"What would I do without you?"

Ruth smiled sweetly. "You'll never know."

Jacob gave Ruth a loving kiss, and then both their eyes were drawn once again to the graveyard outside.

"Strange...strange that it should be today of all days. Thirty years after the Bystander brothers first came into this place...and our lives were forever changed."

Chapter 2

When the call first came from Jacob Bystander I did cartwheels around the room! I was so excited that I couldn't stop bouncing! Never had I imagined such good fortune would come my way. I could envision great doors of opportunity opening to me in the future. This was my shot at all my dreams! The chance to write the autobiography of such a well-known person was almost too good to be true, but it was true and I was sure it would catapult me into fame. How could I pass up such an opportunity?

I did my homework on Jacob Bystander—born June 6, 1942, twin brother of Jonas Bystander, who died in 1964, married to Ruth Lansing in 1966, etc. etc. Facts were easy to find; what the public wanted to know were the details— the secrets in his past—all the juicy stuff. That was what made books sell and made money, and money was my god; it was what I wanted. Money and the power that it gave were the two things in life that counted, or so I thought.

Where would I get the details? I decided to begin with his mother. My research indicated that she was still living in Tulsa, and since I lived in Tulsa as well, it would be a simple matter of making a phone call. Margaret Bystander could provide the details of her son's early years. Once I had interviewed her, I could begin interviewing her son. The call was made, and the events that would change my life forever were set into motion. They were changes that would take me down another path from the one I had chosen and very different from what I had dreamed.

Chapter 3

Margaret Bystander had agreed to grant me an interview. She was a very private woman and generally did not talk to reporters. However, since the interview was in part the result of her son's request for me to write his autobiography, she had consented to see me.

With tape recorder ready to go, I sat in a chair across the table from Margaret and waited for her to begin. She leaned forward, propped her left elbow on the table, and rested her chin on her hand as she looked at me through the top lenses of her glasses. Her piercing green eyes were sharp and observant. It was evident that age had not dimmed her spirit.

"Is there any particular place you would like me to begin?"

"I would like to hear about Jacob's early years—things that happened when he was very young perhaps—things that he will not remember. Whatever you think will be of interest. Maybe a little something about yourself and his father."

Her eyes shifted away from my face and focused on another point in time and space. I could see from the far away look in her face that she was reliving a time gone by. Directly, she shifted in her chair and began to study the gold band on the fourth finger of her right hand. She turned it around a couple of times then began to speak as though I was not even in the room.

"December 7, 1941. President Roosevelt called it a *'day that would live in infamy.'* It is a date that brings to mind images of airplanes, bombs, and ships ablaze. The

11

destruction and loss of life are remembered and recounted every year. But I don't need help to remember Pearl Harbor."

"The events of that day have followed me and shaped my life. Like many others who lost loved ones there, I lost my companion and best friend; I lost my husband."

She stopped .and reflected on the statement before continuing.

"Life for my boys growing up without a father was hard. I knew it would be hard. I had memories to sustain me, but what did they have? I determined to give them as much of their father as I could. Come with me. I want to show you something."

With that, Margaret got up from her chair and motioned to me to follow her. When we reached the living room, she indicated the sofa to me.

"Wait here."

She disappeared through what I assumed was a bedroom door and soon returned dragging behind her a small wooden box. It was only about 24" long, 18" wide and 15" deep. On the top, I could see the name "William David Bystander" carved in the jagged uneven manner of a child. Also, carved on the top were the dates November 6, 1918 and December 7, 1941. It was apparent from the quality of the carving that the second date, the date of William's death, had been carved by a more skilled hand.

"Let me help you with that." I offered but Margaret just waved me aside.

"It's not as heavy as it looks and I'm not as frail as I look."

She stopped in the middle of the floor and with a girlish air sat down in front of the chest. She ran her fingers over the letters carved on the top as though she was caressing her cherished husband's face. Her own face seemed to grow younger with the gesture, while a mixture of sorrow and happiness played with the corners of her mouth and her eyes once again took on that far away look.

"Will made this as a boy. It contains all that is left of him."

When she started to raise the lid, I expected to hear it creak and squeak with age and rusty hinges, but, to my surprise, it didn't make a sound. It opened its window to the past in silence.

Curiosity overpowered me and I joined Margaret on the floor where I could peer in wonder at the treasures it contained.

Margaret's hand went first to a wedding picture. The black and white picture was faded with age and the edges were a little frayed, but the eager young faces of Margaret and William Bystander were unaffected by time.

"This is our wedding picture. We were so young then and had so many dreams and plans for the future." A note of sadness crept into her voice. "We didn't know how little time we had but I don't think it would have made any difference. I can't think of anything that we would have done differently, except for my going to Pearl Harbor with him. You see, when Will shipped out we decided it would be better for me to join him later, after he had found a place for us to live. God only knows what difference my presence might have made."

Margaret's voice trailed off into a thought that she meant more for herself than for anyone else. She paused to ponder the possibilities as she had so many times before, and then shook herself free from her thoughts as she continued with her story.

"We had been married less than a year when Will shipped out for Pearl Harbor. I was supposed to join him there before Christmas...It was not to be. That Christmas of 1941 I spent alone reliving memories of our last moments together."

"I saw his face; I heard his voice. I tried to remember every detail of our parting just as it had been. I wanted to hold onto him and never let him slip away. Sometimes I would spend hours thinking of all the things we had said to each other, and all the things we had left unsaid."

"No matter how many times I replayed our conversations, the results were always the same. I could not change the past. My thoughts were filled with 'if onlys.' My one conciliation was that Will had received my last letter the day before he died."

Margaret tenderly set the picture back in its place and picked up a box tied with a faded ribbon.

"I kept all the letters he sent me from Pearl Harbor. There weren't that many but I treasure each one."

She untied the ribbon on the box and set the lid aside. She carefully picked up the letter on top. The paper was brown with age and starting to crack and crumble on the edges.

"I shudder when I recall how I almost didn't send this letter. When I found out that I was pregnant, my first thought was of Will. All the way home, I tried to picture his face and his reaction when he heard the news! I wanted to tell him in person not in a letter, but my excitement was too great to be contained." Margaret held the letter tenderly in her hands, being careful not to damage it. She looked at me as she continued.

"My hands flew across the pages as I wrote Will of my joy, excitement, hopes, and fears. I poured my heart out in this letter and when the news of his death arrived...I thanked God that I had not waited."

I could see water collecting in her eyes and a lump was beginning to form in my throat.

"When the telegram I feared came, I held it in my hands and cried. Every word I had written in that last letter came flooding back. I was struck with the realization that if I had not mailed that letter, Will would have died without knowing he was going to be a father...perhaps it's silly, but...I think his knowing somehow made losing him more bearable."

Margaret blinked away the tears in her eyes as she gently put the letter back in its box and retied the ribbon.

"When the boys were growing up, they would often go through this box and read the letters. They thought I didn't know they read them, but I did. They would look at the pictures and touch his things. I made it available to them. It was all they had...I prayed it was enough."

Margaret waved her hand across the top of the open box.

"Every item in here has a story, a tale. Will's friends contributed some of the items. I used to sit with my boys in the floor, as we are now, recounting the history behind every piece. When they were old enough, they would go through it on their own whenever they wanted to be with their father."

The lump in my throat grew larger and threatened to choke me as water sprang to my eyes without my permission. I had not come prepared for the image, which

Margaret painted for me of two little boys grasping for bits and pieces of their dead father. This was a side of Jacob and Jonas Bystander that was absent from my research.

"I'd like to hear some more stories if you have time to share them with me?"

She looked at me with those perceptive green eyes and smiled.

"It is not my time which is in question, but yours. Do you have time to listen?"

"That's why I'm here." I said confidently. I could not imagine leaving yet with such a spellbinding storyteller ready to open the windows of the past to me.

"Please, I want to hear more." With that, I twisted around on the floor, crossing my legs and propping my elbows on my knees, ready to hang on every word. Margaret flashed another grin in my direction. I suspected, rather than knew, that she regarded me as an eager child intent on a bedtime story. She began her journey again into the pages of time, but this time she took me with her.

"I had mailed that last letter to Will on November 28. The mail was slow and I learned later that he received it on December 6...the day before he died. On that fateful day, I had gone to church as usual. Service had just finished and I was visiting with friends before going home, when one of the little boys came running into the church and said the Japanese had attacked Pearl Harbor."

Margaret shrugged her shoulders and shook her head. The smile was gone from her face.

"Everyone thought it was a joke at first, but he insisted he had just heard it on a car radio. We still didn't believe him. Never the less, we followed him outside to the car where the radio could be heard spilling forth the excited voice of the announcer. Other children were gathered around the car motionless and silent. Their faces turned instinctively to us as we approached. Some were white with fear, others were like stone—frozen in unbelief—still others were wrapped in grief with little trails of tears running down their cheeks. One look at their faces said that it was true…"

Margaret paused in her story. I waited patiently until she was ready to continue.

"I watched as parents gathered children; husbands and wives clung to each other, and sweethearts exchanged worried looks. For myself…I stood alone for a few minutes just listening…remembering that letter. A thousand thoughts and images flashed through my mind and I couldn't help placing my hand on my stomach and…"

Margaret's voice began to quiver ever so slightly at this point as her hands moved instinctively to her stomach. "And I remembered our baby. I wasn't alone after all. I tore myself away from the blaring radio and went back inside the church to pray. God would be my source of hope and comfort."

At this point, the lump in my throat became too much for me, and the tears I had been fighting won the battle.

Chapter 4

Nothing could have prepared Margaret for the agonizing wait that followed the first news reports of the attack. The days of waiting crawled by unbearably slow. She did her best to stay busy but there are only so many times you can sweep a floor or make a bed. Daily, Margaret found herself drawn to her collection of letters and pictures. She sat in the floor by their bed and reread each of Will's letters and looked at the few pictures she had of him. She hoped he would be among those who had been spared and prayed that the answer would come soon. The Navy would notify her if he had been killed but she would have to wait for a letter from him if he were safe. She waited in dread of the knock on the door that never came.

Finally, in the late hours of one of those many days, exhaustion overcame her thoughts at last, and Margaret crawled up on her bed and fell asleep. It was not a restful sleep because her dreams were filled with images of Will. She saw him walking by the lake with his fishing pole over his shoulder as she had seen him do so many times before. He stopped and began to gather wood for a fire. He had so enjoyed camping by the lake and cooking his catch over an open flame. She watched as he began to chop some of the wood into smaller pieces. The chopping grew louder until Margaret realized it wasn't Will's chopping she heard but something outside her dream.

She struggled against the sound. She didn't want to wake up; she wanted to hang onto her dream, but the pounding persisted until she was forced to open her eyes. Only half awake, Margaret looked at the clock and saw it was 8:00 a.m. Then the knocking came again. Someone was at the door. Hurriedly, she went to see who it was.

Poised with her hand on the doorknob, Margaret knew even before she saw him, who was standing on the other side of that door. Her fingers were stiff and cold as they moved mechanically to turn the knob. Her heart was pounding and her knees suddenly felt too weak to support her weight.

The man from the telegraph office looked very somber as he held the telegram out to her. The only thing he said was, "I'm sorry." And then he walked away and left Margaret standing alone with the telegram in her hand. What she had feared was now confirmed.

She watched the man leave in stunned silence. The telegram in her hand bore the unmistakable greeting from the United States Department of the Navy. It could mean only one thing—Will was dead. Margaret didn't need to read it to know. Yet, it didn't seem real. Was she supposed to accept his death based on a piece of paper? What if there had been a mistake? Mistakes do happen. How did they know he was dead? Had someone identified his body? Where was his body if he was dead?

Unwilling to accept the finality of the telegram, questions began to flood Margaret's mind but she didn't have any answers. At last, she reasoned that if Will were alive, he would write to her and let her know. If she didn't hear from him…Margaret didn't want to believe he was gone, but the telegram was all too final.

Very slowly Margaret turned and closed the door behind her. What little energy and strength she had possessed, drained away leaving her weak and listless. She found her way to her favorite rocking chair and collapsed. She sat there rocking the rest of the day, lost in the past and unwilling to think of the future. Day passed into evening and evening passed into night. When night eventually gave way to a new day, it found Margaret still sitting in her rocker clutching the telegram in her hand.

It was like a bad dream that didn't go away. She wanted to wake up but couldn't. What was she going to do now? Margaret looked around the room at all the familiar furnishings. Each one held a memory. Each item represented bits and pieces of her life with Will. Everything she looked at reminded her of him.

He couldn't be gone! He just couldn't be—not now! Not when she was going to have a baby. It wasn't fair!

Margaret jumped out of her rocker and ran to the bedroom. "It isn't fair, God! How could you let him be killed? It isn't fair!" Margaret threw herself on the bed and allowed the tears that she had held back to flow freely. Great sobs racked her body as her grief ran unchecked for hours.

When Margaret could cry no more, she sat up and hugged her pillow to her chest. She looked across the room and saw her reflection in the mirror. Her eyes were puffy and her nose was red but Margaret didn't notice. Instead, she saw herself holding a baby in her arms. Life wasn't fair...but God was merciful. Will was gone but she still had their baby. She would be able to hold onto it. She would be strong for their baby.

Margaret suddenly felt very determined and very hungry. She washed her face, changed her clothes, and looked for something to eat. She couldn't change the past but she could still influence the future and she would start right now by taking good care of their child.

Chapter 5

Margaret sent letter after letter to various agencies trying to find out more about William's death, but answers never came. She couldn't find out what had become of him. Where was he? Was he buried at Pearl Harbor? What was she supposed to do now? Should she have a funeral or a memorial service? Should she wait until his body was shipped home...if it was going to be shipped home? Without answers, it was hard for Margaret to accept that William was dead. Somewhere in the back of her mind, she kept hoping that the telegram was a mistake and William had not contacted her because of military secrecy.

One day about a month after the attack, a small package arrived from Pearl Harbor. When Margaret first saw the return address, her heart began to race. The handwriting was not that of Will, still, she thought perhaps he had been injured and someone else had addressed the package for him. Inside, she found a letter and a gold watch. Ignoring the watch, she hurriedly opened the letter and began to read. The first few words erased all doubt as to the sender. It was not Will.

Calm replaced the previous excitement. The smile faded from Margaret's face. She sat at the kitchen table wrapped in the warmth of the afternoon sun as it poured through the window and began to read.

Lillian Delaney

My Dear Mrs. Bystander,

Words at such a time as this seem hollow and do little to sooth your pain, but I wanted to share with you the events surrounding William's death. Perhaps it will help in the years to come to know what happened.

I had only known William a short time. He came to chapel on a regular basis. He was my most faithful attendant. We would talk on Sunday afternoons about his hometown of Seneca, Missouri. He told stories of walking the hills in search of blackberries and wading in the creek that runs through the town. According to William, the fishing at Twin Bridges was better than here, but it could not compare in beauty with the Pacific Ocean. Still, the hills of home were the most precious place on earth to him because of you.

Mostly he talked about you and how much he looked forward to you joining him here. He was sure that you and my wife would become the best of friends.

The morning of the attack, William had come to service early. He had received your letter the day before and was bursting with excitement. He didn't want to wait until after services to tell me. We were in the Chapel making plans for your move here when we heard the planes. We rushed to the windows to see what was going on. In the distance, we saw great rolling pillars of smoke and flames.

Explosion followed explosion, then more pillars shot into the sky. We stood mesmerized by what we saw for what seemed like several minutes, but in reality it was only a few seconds.

We heard the deafening sound of an airplane bearing down on us. It was strafing the ground with its machine gun. Somewhere in the distance I heard William shout, "Get down!" then I was knocked to the floor. At first, I thought I had been shot, but I realized that the blow I had felt had come from William. I had stood frozen by the scene outside unable to move. He had lunged at me when he saw that I was not moving. He saved my life.

I struggled to move but William was sprawled across me. I shook him but he didn't respond. When I rolled him over, his uniform showed the stains from the blood. Your letter lay on the floor where it had fallen when he rushed to my aid.

I looked from the letter back to William and wept. I wept for the father who would never know his child. I wept for the child who would never know its father. I wept for the wife who would face the future without her mate. But most of all...I wept for myself.

It should have been me laying there not him. I should have been the one to sacrifice not him. I am the one who chose to commit my life to the service of others. But it wasn't me whose time had come; it was William's. Because of his act of unselfishness, I can dream of the future and go on serving others.

I can't change or undo what has happened. No matter how many times I replay that day in my mind, the results are always the same.

William's legacy to his child is his final act of heroism. He gave his life to save another. I have included with this letter his gold pocket watch. I had it engraved with his name and the date of his death. It is my prayer that the inscription will help to ease the pain of your loss and, somehow, express my never-ending gratitude.

God bless you and keep you both in the years ahead.

Reverend Robert J. Lansing

Tears formed little pools in Margaret's eyes, blurring her vision. Several times she wiped them away in order to see the words that Reverend Lansing had penned. When she had finished the letter, she held the gold watch gently in the palm of her hand as though, somehow, it was connected to Will. She pressed the lever that opened the watch. The inscription inside read:

WILLIAM DAVID BYSTANDER

GAVE HIS LIFE UNSELFISHLY
TO SAVE THE LIFE OF ANOTHER

DECEMBER 7, 1941

Margaret clutched the watch in both hands and clasped it to her heart as she allowed herself to sob uncontrollably. A cloud had passed between the sun and the window, and the warm glow of day had been replaced with gloomy shadows. The numbness of disbelief gave way to reality. Having read the words of Reverend Lansing, Margaret could no longer hope for a mistake or pray for a miracle. The watch and the letter were final.

Chapter 6

News travels quickly in a small town. It wasn't long before everyone knew of Margaret's loss. At the post office, a bulletin board bore the names of those who were lost in battle. Will's name was first on the list, but he was not to be the last. As time went on, other names were added. The town seemed to be in a constant state of mourning.

In the midst of the mourning; however, an occasional bit of joy could be found. So it was for Margaret as the time for the birth of her baby grew near. It was June 6, 1942 and the war in Europe was raging.

Margaret was preparing for church when the pains started. She had had pains before and, since she wasn't due yet, she decided to go on to church. However, the pains grew in intensity and closeness all through the service. By the end of the service, she could barely walk.

Sadie, an older lady from the church, helped Margaret get back home. It was too far to the nearest hospital; Margaret had waited too long. It would be better for the baby to be born at home than in the car.

"You lay down and try to relax." Sadie coaxed Margaret. "Pastor is calling the doctor and he will be here soon. I'll be right here with you." Sadie helped Margaret change her clothes and get into bed.

Margaret was feeling very sick and weak, and was grateful for the help of her friend. Little beads of sweat were beginning to appear on Margaret's forehead as she looked at Sadie with a helpless and pleading expression.

Sadie wiped her face with a damp cloth and spoke in soft soothing tones. "There, there, it won't be long before you'll have a wonderful treasure to hold in your arms and you'll forget all about the pain."

Another pain began and Margaret winced.

"Don't fight it, Maggie. Hold my hand and squeeze it when the pain starts. Concentrate on my hand and not the pain." Sadie sat in a chair next to the bed holding Margaret's small hand in her large one and started on a tale of her own.

"Did I ever tell you about the day my Johnny was born?"

Margaret looked at Sadie and squeaked out a weak reply. "No."

"Well, it was January and bitter cold. We had had one ice storm after another for three weeks. The house was almost completely bare of food. I was afraid if I waited any longer for the roads to clear, the baby would come and then I would really be in trouble. I could find myself with no food and a newborn baby. You see...I was alone too. Johnny's father was in France." A touch of sadness crept into Sadie's face. "He was killed in World War I."

Margaret knew this of course. Everyone knew how Sadie's husband died in WWI and now her son Johnny was fighting in World War II. The church as a whole prayed every week for those who were gone to fight.

"Anyway," Sadie brushed away her sadness; "I walked the two miles to the store and bought a few things—only what I could carry. While I was walking home, the pains started. I made it home safely, put my groceries away, and then walked to a neighbor's house. By the time I got there, Johnny was practically born. They sent for a doctor, but he didn't arrive in time." Sadie smiled. "I guess that little walk really got things going."

Sadie continued to talk about Johnny and his childhood. Margaret listened but really didn't hear very much. She was just thankful for Sadie's presence.

After about an hour, Margaret looked at Sadie with concern.

"Sadie?"

"Yes, Maggie?"

"I want to pray that everything will be okay. I'm worried about the baby. I couldn't stand to lose it too."

Sadie patted Margaret on the hand and wiped her face again. She swallowed hard and steadied her voice before answering. "Of course we'll pray." With that, Sadie held both Margaret's young hands in her two strong ones and prayed for God to watch over and protect both mother and child. Just as they finished praying, the doctor arrived.

The next couple of hours went quickly and by 4:00 p.m., Jonas Eli Bystander had arrived.

"We have a boy!" The doctor announced. There was a general round of congratulations as everyone in the room declared him a beautiful baby. Just as Margaret was prepared to rest and hold her new son, she felt the contractions begin again.

"Whoa! Wait a minute, we have another baby!" The doctor quickly started giving orders to his nurse and his face took on a worried expression. The room grew strangely quiet as everyone began to speak in whispers. Margaret noticed the change and wondered what was wrong. After a few minutes, the doctor calmly announced, "You have another boy, Margaret."

The smile that Maggie shared at the announcement quickly faded as she realized the baby was not crying. He was not breathing and Margaret watched in horror as a nurse took the tiny blue and gray body and began to rub it and clean its nose. All eyes, but those of the doctor, were on the nurse and lifeless baby. Sadie could be heard praying quietly next to Margaret.

It wasn't long before a weak sounding little whimper was heard coming from the direction of the nurse and the infant. Then it became louder and stronger until it was a full-grown wail. A general sigh of relief swept over the room, and faces that only moments before were shrouded in grief, visibly relaxed and smiled. A round of relieved laughter burst forth mixed with congratulations for the new mother.

The second boy was promptly named Jacob William Bystander and joined his brother Jonas in a warm bed close to his mother's side. Margaret looked at her two boys with a heart overflowing with love and pride. She studied their little faces and marveled at how much they looked like their father.

"They sure do look a lot like Will." Sadie echoed Maggie's thoughts.

"Yes, they do." Maggie's voice was barely audible and sounded tired.

Sadie looked at Maggie and noticed one lonely tear that was trailing down the side of her face. A mixture of sorrow and joy lingered in her eyes. She patted Maggie's hand. "You did a good job and I know those boys are going to be a blessing to you."

Margaret wiped away the tear with one hand as she whispered, "and I will restore to you the years that the locust has eaten…the Lord has repaid twice for that which was lost."

The room grew strangely quiet again, as it became apparent that something was wrong. The look on the doctor's face was worried and he talked to his nurse in urgent tones. Sadie looked from the doctor to Maggie. Her face was growing pale and ashen. She seemed to be struggling to keep her eyes open.

"What's wrong?" Sadie wanted to know.

"I can't get the bleeding to stop."

The situation was growing critical very fast. Sadie kissed Maggie on the forehead and quickly left the room with a backward glance at the new mother and her two babies. In the next room Sadie joined with other friends from church, who had gathered during the course of the day. They got on their knees together and began to pray as they had never prayed before.

Maggie was barely aware of Sadie's absence. She felt so tired. Her eyelids became too heavy to lift, so she stopped trying to open them. She tried to move her hand but it was too heavy. She laid there peacefully resting and listening to the conversations around her. The nurse took her blood pressure—60 over 40. In the back of her mind, Maggie knew that was not good. She thought to herself, *'My life is slipping away. I'm dying, but I'm not afraid. I feel so calm and peaceful.'*

The anxiety in the doctor's voice was more intense. Maggie could hear him praying and knew that she had nothing to fear. She felt only peace. Then she remembered her two baby boys. Who would care for them? It would be so easy to just drift into the next world where there was no pain or sadness and Will was waiting, but what of their two babies? She needed to live for them. For them, she wanted to live.

A few moments later Margaret heard an excited doctor proclaim, "Thank you, Lord! Yes! Thank you, God!" The crisis had passed.

Sadie had re-entered the room and was patting Maggie on the cheeks trying to wake her. "Maggie, Maggie, can you hear me? Maggie, I need to know if you can hear me?"

Margaret could not open her eyes. The lids were too heavy. She couldn't move her arms or turn her head, but she mustered all the strength she had and answered Sadie.

"Yes." It was a very faint sound, but it was enough to let the doctor and Sadie know that Margaret was still with them.

Before he left, the doctor explained that Margaret would live, but recovery would be slow. She would need help for several months as she rebuilt her strength. Sadie and all the other church friends who had prayed for her promised to help. Until that moment, Margaret had never realized how much she was loved.

In the days and weeks that followed, Margaret grew stronger and better able to care for her sons. They were a joy and a delight to her heart. The friends who had prayed for her on the day of their birth stood by her side as they grew. Their constant prayers reminded her that she didn't have to stand alone, and made that difficult time of her life somewhat easier to bear.

Chapter 7

Margaret stood silently and stared at the deep blue of the lake. The early morning light shimmered across the water and the slight breeze sent ripples racing to touch the rocks on the shore. In a few more months the lake would be overtaken by fishermen...but not this day. It was cold, but what did that matter? Long after this day was over and the cold was forgotten, Margaret would be alone with her memories.

A small wooden chest crafted by the inexperienced hands of a small boy many years before, sat before her. William had carved his name in the lid of the box as well as his birthday. A friend had added the date of his death. It had been his box of treasures. Now it would serve as a treasury for memories—bits and pieces of a father seen only through the items it contained.

Margaret had already placed several items inside—their wedding picture, his letters from Pearl Harbor, his favorite pair of moccasins, and her letters to him. Reverend Lansing had recovered them and sent them to her shortly after Will's death. Today, others would come and add their gifts to the chest—individual pieces of his life. Memories and stories attached to objects. Each item would include a note from the giver telling why the object was special. William would speak to his sons through the lives he had touched.

The group which had assembled for the memorial service was small—only a handful of close friends. Most of William's classmates had moved away years ago or had joined the military as he had. Now they were fighting in the war and could not attend. It was just as well. There was nothing to see. When they were first married, William had made her promise to have him cremated if he should die first. He wanted to be remembered as he had lived not as a cold and stiff corpse in a coffin.

Margaret had kept her promise. William's ashes now rested in a blue urn with puffs of white clouds flouting around the rim while an eagle with wings spread wide seemed to soar into the distant heavens. Margaret had thought of William's strong free spirit the moment she saw it. She knew in her heart that—like the eagle—he was flying through heavenly places right now.

"We're ready to begin, Margaret."

Margaret was shaken from her thoughts by the Reverend Lightfoot. He was the pastor of the small Indian Church to which William and Margaret belonged. He wore his hair in two very long braids and lived in a teepee—when the weather permitted. If it got too cold or too wet, he moved into a small log cabin he had built in the hills around Seneca.

Reverend Lightfoot offered his arm to Margaret as they made their way up the winding stone steps, which led to the "Indian Territory Cultural Center." Cultural Center—the name held high expectations for the future, but for now it was a log cabin situated in a clearing on a bluff overlooking the lake.

Local inhabitants had donated the land and cut the trees themselves from which the building was made. Even the artifacts, pictures, and assorted newspaper clippings had been donated by the people in surrounding towns. The Center wasn't fancy or large, but it spoke of their pride in their heritage and their people. Even William had helped with the construction of the Center; that is why Margaret had chosen this place for his memorial service.

Margaret joined Sadie on a rough hand hewn log bench. Sadie was holding Jonas on one knee and Jacob on the other. At six months, they could be a handful, but today they seemed to sense the solemn mood of the occasion and were unusually quiet. Maggie reached for Jacob, and then offered her free arm to Jonas. As she held them, they snuggled close under their mother's protective wings.

Reverend Lightfoot placed the urn on top of the chest as he began to speak.

"Margaret has asked me to conduct the proceedings here today. I could stand here and say many things about William but I won't. Those of us who knew Will understood his kind and thoughtful nature. For those of you who perhaps did not know that side of him, I am going to tell a story."

He settled into his story telling tone of voice and walked around the small room as he spoke. All eyes, however, were focused on the pictures of Will, which hung on display behind the urn. As the story progressed, William himself seemed to be speaking.

"About three years ago, Will came to me and said he wanted to be baptized. I asked him 'why.' He replied, *'Because I want to follow Christ in baptism and as a sign of my faith in the Creator.'* We planned the ceremony for dawn the following week. The night before, we camped on the bank of the lake just below these cliffs. As we sat around the campfire that night, Will began to share with me his favorite tribal story. This is the story he shared."

There was once a little mouse that was not like the other mice. All the other mice walked through the fields with their noses to the ground sniffing for something to eat, but not this little mouse. He wanted to see the world so he was always jumping as high as he could to see above the tall grass.

Once Little Jumping Mouse saw a great river and he said "Oh, how much I would like to cross that river and see what is on the other side but I am too small." Another time Little Jumping Mouse saw the big mountains and said, "I would like very much to go to the top of the mountains. I could see much of the world from there."

Then one day while Little Jumping Mouse was making his way through the field, he met a buffalo stumbling through the grass. Little Jumping Mouse asked Mr. Buffalo, "Why are you stumbling through the brush Mr. Buffalo?" Mr. Buffalo replied, "Because I'm blind." Then Little Jumping mouse answered, "Poor Mr. Buffalo, is there anything I can do for you?" "Nothing," said Mr. Buffalo, "unless you can take out your eyes and give them to me so I can see."

Without even thinking, Little Jumping Mouse pulled out one of his eyes and gave it to Mr. Buffalo. Mr. Buffalo put the eye in his head and he could see. He cried, "Oh! Thank you Little Jumping Mouse! I can see again! Is there anything I can do for you?"

Little Jumping Mouse replied, "Oh, yes! I have always wanted to cross the great river and see what is on the other side."

"Climb upon my shoulder, Little Jumping Mouse and I will carry you across."

So Little Jumping Mouse climbed upon Mr. Buffalo's shoulder and he swam across the great river.

Now that Little Jumping Mouse was on the other side of the river, he continued to jump high above the tall grass to look around. There was much to see.

One day he was in the field with the other mice when one of the mice began to yell, "Hide! A wolf is coming and he will eat us!" All the mice began to run and hide—all except Little Jumping Mouse. He jumped above the tall grass to see and sure enough, there was a wolf coming. But he was stumbling along slowly because he was blind.

Little Jumping Mouse felt so sorry for Mr. Wolf that he asked him, "Mr. Wolf is there anything I can do for you?"

"Nothing," said Mr. Wolf, "unless you could give me one of your eyes so that I could see."

Without even thinking, Little Jumping Mouse reached up, pulled out his other eye, and gave it to Mr. Wolf. Now Mr. Wolf could see again but Little Jumping Mouse was blind.

Mr. Wolf said, "Oh, thank you Little Jumping Mouse! I can see again, but now you are blind. Is there anything I can do for you?"

"Yes," said Little Jumping Mouse, "I have always wanted to go to the top of those mountains.

"Hop on my shoulders Little Jumping Mouse and I will take you there." Mr. Wolf answered. So Little Jumping Mouse hopped on Mr. Wolf's shoulders and off he ran to the top of the mountain.

When he reached the top, Mr. Wolf sat Little Jumping Mouse down on the bank of a great lake and left him there. But since he couldn't see, Little Jumping Mouse could not go anywhere so he just sat there and waited. Pretty soon,

Mr. Eagle swooped down out of the sky and snatched up Little Jumping Mouse in his talons and soared high into the sky. Little Jumping Mouse screamed in terror. "Oh no! I'm going to be lunch for this Eagle!"

"I'm not going to eat you Little Jumping Mouse." Said Mr. Eagle. "Because of your kindness to the Buffalo and the Wolf, you are going to be brother to the Eagle." With that, the Eagle let go of Little Jumping Mouse and he began to tumble and fall to the Earth.

As he was falling, Little Jumping Mouse began to grow bigger, and feathers began to appear on his body. He could see again as he soared through the sky with his new wings. He could see farther than he had ever been able to see before as he flew over the mountains, because now he was brother to the Eagle. He was a hawk.

At the conclusion of the story, four men seated around a drum began to beat the drum and chant in unison. There were no distinct words, but the hearts of those who listened understood the language they spoke. When they had concluded, Reverend Lightfoot again spoke to the people.

"This chest that you see was made by Will. In it Maggie has place several items of significance connected to him." The Reverend placed the story of the Little Jumping Mouse on top of the chest. "I am adding this to the collection. In the years ahead, Maggie will be able to read this story to her sons and they will come to know the heart of the father who has gone ahead. Those of you who have something to add, come now with your gifts."

The Reverend took a seat to the side as the people came one at a time and placed their treasures on the box. There was a black felt hat that Will had given to a neighbor, a pair of moccasins he had made for Granny Whitebear, his favorite hunting knife, and a beaded buckskin vest that he had given to Sadie's son, Johnny, only a week before he left. Some of the items he had given away as gifts in the hard years before the war; others he had given to close friends just before he left for Pearl Harbor. It was as though he had known he would not be coming back.

The giving of gifts was over. Margaret handed the boys back to Sadie, took the urn from the top of the chest and led the small group of mourners outside. She walked in silence to the edge of the bluff and stood looking out over the lake. No one spoke a word. Even the wind seemed to hold its breath in anticipation of what would happen next. Seven veterans from WWI stood at attention with their guns at their sides. A bugler waited for the orders to play, and an American flag flew at half-mast in front of the Center.

Margaret slowly opened the urn, set the lid carefully on the ground, and held the urn at arms length over the edge of the cliff. Far below, she could see the water splashing and jumping at the rocks. In the distance the lake stretched for miles as it sat patiently waiting for her to fulfill this one last request.

The time had come. Margaret tipped the urn ever so gently and the ashes began to rain softly down upon the face of the water. A sudden gust of wind caught some and whisked them away to an unknown destination.

At last, the urn was empty and Margaret stooped to retrieve the lid. She returned it to its proper place and stood with her face lifted toward heaven. With her eyes closed, Margaret breathed a final goodbye. "Until that day when God shall sound his trumpet and all that has been scattered shall be called from the Four Corners of the world and we shall be together again." One small tear found its way from behind her closed eyes and trickled down her cheek. She bravely wiped it away before turning to face the gathering of family and friends.

The bugler raised his bugle to his lips and the lonesome and forlorn melody of "Taps" filled the air. When he had finished, the order was given for the veterans to present arms and fire. Three times, they fired. Three times the hills echoed their salute. Finally, the American flag was lowered, meticulously folded in its traditional triangle, and presented to Margaret. The officer presenting the flag saluted her, then turned with a snap and marched back to join his men.

The service was now finished. People began to mill around and visit. Margaret, however, searched the ground for the twenty-one spent shell casings. When she had found them all, she put them in her pocket. Later that day she would add them to the chest of memories. In the years ahead, she would explain their significance to her boys and recount for them the events of this day.

Chapter 8

The years slowly slipped past. As Jonas and Jacob prepared to celebrate their fourth birthday, the war in Europe was a memory. The newspapers and newsreels were no longer filled with war and death. The end to the war had also brought an end to the long list of names at the post office.

The years had drawn Margaret and Sadie closer together. They shared many common bonds. They had both lost husbands in war, they were single mothers, and they both loved Jonas and Jacob.

Sadie had become a devoted godmother to the boys. She watched them while Margaret was working and told them stories about their father as a boy. She especially liked to tell stories that included her son Johnny. Johnny and William had been friends as boys and had had many adventures together.

Jonas and Jacob always listened with intense interest, but sometimes wondered why Sadie seemed sad after telling her stories. After all, Johnny wasn't dead. He lived at home with his mother and played games with them. He liked to give them piggyback rides and tickle them. They didn't understand that Johnny had come home from the war, but the war had not been left behind. It had come home with him.

He lived somewhere in the past and often sat staring into space with a blank empty look on his face. His sleep was seldom peaceful. Instead, it was filled with restlessness, and bad dreams. After a bad night, he would withdraw more into his childlike world—a peaceful carefree time before the war. Sometimes, he would forget and call one of the boys William. Other times, he would come into his "right-mind" and start crying, or shaking, or both. Those were the worst moments and were always followed by a period of silence.

On this day, Sadie watched the boys playing in the yard as she put icing on a birthday cake. Her son, Johnny, sat nearby tinkering with an old tricycle he had found in a ditch or a dump somewhere. A slight twinge of sadness crept into her heart and threatened to cast a shadow over the happiness of the occasion.

She reminded herself how lucky she was to have her son back safe and—sound was what Sadie had thought but the word stuck in her throat. Johnny was only "sound" in body. His mind was not. Shell shock was what the doctors called it. Whatever the name, Sadie knew that her son had not come home from the war. He had been left behind somewhere on a battlefield in Europe.

Johnny was like a child again. He played with the twins almost every day. He gave them piggyback rides and rolled in the leaves with them. He had not forgotten many of the things he had learned, like driving a car or working with tools, but he wanted no part of the adult world.

Today, Johnny knew it was Jonas and Jacob's birthday. He was fixing something for them. He sanded off the rust, replaced missing screws and bolts, and then checked the handlebars to make sure they moved smoothly. Next, he dragged out an old wagon. He attached it to the back of the tricycle. All This activity made the boys curious about what Johnny was doing. They came to see what he had made.

"Whatcha doin' Johnny?" Jacob was the first to speak.

"Fixin a tricycle for my special friends."

"What's a tricycle?" Jonas stood looking puzzled at the strange thing with three wheels.

"It's somethin' you ride on like this." Johnny sat on the seat that was far too small for his man-size body. The handlebars rested between his knees as he gripped them and pretended to be peddling. He was a funny sight with his elbows pointed out, his back arched, and his head hunched down.

"You peddle the wheels like this and then you can move like the wind!" He made an exaggerated whooshing sound and the brothers began to laugh. Johnny just looked at them and laughed, too. Then he hopped off and said, "Happy Birthday! It's for my two best buddies!" He leaned over and patted the wagon with his hand. "This is so one can peddle and one can ride. When you get tired, you can change places. This way you can always stick together and help each other."

Sadie watched the scene from her window and smiled. It didn't matter that her son had not come home the same as he had left. All that was good and kind and gentle was still Johnny. He was still a joy to her heart and a blessing to those around him.

A tear threatened to cloud Sadie's eye, but she quickly wiped it away with her apron. She refused to let anything dampen this day. She walked out onto the porch and stood gazing at the three boys. Johnny was teaching Jacob how to peddle the tricycle and to steer at the same time. Each boy took turns while the other watched. Soon, they were ready to try it with one boy riding in the wagon. In no time at all, they were going all over the yard and up and down the drive with ease.

"Look, Johnny!" Jonas shouted.

"I kin do it! I kin do it!"

Johnny smiled and waved. "I knew you could!"

About that time, Sadie saw Maggie walking up the drive. She was home from work. The boys saw her about the same time. They jumped off their new toy and raced toward her with excited shouts.

"Mom! Mom!"

"Look what Johnny gave us!" Both boys were jumping up and down tugging at Margaret's arms and pointing in the direction of the tricycle with the wagon attached.

"Ain't it great, Mom!"

"Isn't it great." Margaret corrected.

"Ya think it's great, too, Mom?" Jonas rushed on. "It's fur our birthday! Johnny fixed it fur us! See what we kin do!" With that, both boys dropped their mother's hands and raced back to their new toy as fast as their little legs would carry them.

Margaret joined Sadie on the porch swing.

"I hope you don't mind. John found that old thing somewhere and dragged it home. He wanted to do something for the boys for their birthday." Sadie handed Margaret a glass of water.

"Of course I don't mind. The boys love him and he helps fill a void in their lives."

Sadie nodded her head in agreement. After a slight pause, she added, "They fill a void in his life, too."

Both women sat quietly for a time watching the two little boys and the one big one race up and down the drive. Johnny would trot beside the two little boys encouraging them, and giving an occasional extra push. Margaret smiled as the boys traded places and started off again as fast as they could go. Every once in awhile the one in the wagon would hang his leg over the side and give a little push to help move things along. As she watched them, Maggie couldn't help being proud of her boys. They shared a special bond that grew stronger with each passing year.

Chapter 9

Christmas, 1949—Jonas and Jacob were seven years old. Where had the time gone? Maggie could hardly believe her boys were so big. It seemed like only yesterday that they had taken their first steps. Now they were in the second grade and romping through the hills fishing and hunting with Johnny.

They looked and acted more and more like Will everyday. Their dark hair had grown long and straight, and they wore it in a braid down their backs. The dark eyes they had been born with were beginning to lighten and change color. In spite of their blue eyes, they were the image of Will in more than just appearance; their kind hearts had won the admiration of the local inhabitants.

They were always together. They delivered newspapers, cleared sidewalks and porches of snow, ran errands, and fed livestock. They worked as one. Many times, they worked without pay. Widows, the elderly, and the Church benefited from the generous nature of the Bystander boys. They understood what it meant to be poor and in need. They knew what it meant to go without things. They knew, perhaps, too much for their young years.

Maggie had done her best over the years, but her job paid little and the small VA benefit she drew could never quite make up the difference between her income and the family needs.

Christmas was always a particularly hard time. Maggie wanted so much to make it a happy time for her boys. She vowed every year to start early and set aside enough money to buy gifts. Somehow, it never seemed to work out the way she planned.

This year was no different—except, perhaps, a little worse. Christmas was almost here and Maggie was juggling bills in order to put presents under the tree and provide a nice dinner on Christmas day. With only two days left, Maggie sat early in the morning and studied their Christmas tree in the corner. It was such a beautiful tree. Her boys had gone up in the hills and found it. They cut it down and pulled it over the rough terrain tied onto the wagon Johnny had given them on their fourth birthday. Together, with Johnny's help, they had put it on a platform and made it secure.

It was decorated with homemade ornaments that they had made in school, as well as some they had made with Johnny and Sadie in past years. Here and there were old ornaments left over from Maggie's childhood and one or two from Will's.

This was supposed to be a happy time. Yet, Maggie's heart was heavy. She looked at the empty space under the tree. She knew that Jonas and Jacob expected something to appear magically before Christmas morning. How far could she make the money stretch? Perhaps some crayons and paper could be managed. At least they would have a package to open.

Maggie fought the tears that threatened to overtake her. She would have to teach them that Christmas was more than presents, and hope that they understood. Still, it would be nice to be able to provide for them better.

As Maggie was thinking on these things, a knock came at her door. It was the Reverend Lightfoot.

"Hello, Maggie. Are the boys up yet?"

"No, I let them sleep a little later since they're out of school."

"In that case, I would like to talk to you outside for a minute so they won't accidentally overhear us."

Maggie grabbed her coat from the hook by the door and stepped outside. "What is it Reverend? Have they done something wrong?"

"Oh, no, nothing like that." The Reverend smiled as he continued. "Maggie, we know that things are very hard for you and the boys. We, at the Church, know you work hard, and that the boys work hard, too. Well...we wanted to bless you as much as you have blessed us. So, we took up a collection and we want to buy gifts for you and the boys for Christmas."

Maggie stood without speaking. She hardly knew what to think. This was so unexpected.

"What we need from you are some ideas as to what the boys would like and what you would like as well."

"I...don't hardly know what to say—toys I suppose, maybe a new fishing pole. I...I don't really know." Maggie thought about the shiny new bicycles they had seen in town. Jonas and Jacob had pressed their faces against the store window and talked excitedly about them. How much they would like to have one of those bicycles! They had long since outgrown their tricycle and shared a rusty old girls bike that Johnny had found somewhere. It got them around, but...to have a new bike—blue for Jacob and green for Jonas—now that would be a dream come true.

Maggie couldn't bring herself to ask. It would be too much to expect. "I'm sure that whatever you give them they will love. It is the thought that counts."

"And what about you, Maggie?"

"I don't need much, maybe a new dress for Church?"

The Reverend smiled again and pressed Maggie's small hand between his big ones. "We'll see what we can do. Now don't tell the boys. We will come by on Christmas Eve, after they go to bed, with your gifts. Okay?"

"Okay. Thank you, Reverend. You don't know what this means to us." Maggie's voice began to crack and her lips quivered as little pools of water collected in her eyes.

Maggie watched Reverend Lightfoot drive away before returning to the house. The clouds that had threatened her day were gone. She looked with anticipation for Christmas Eve now instead of with sorrow. The kindness of others was going to make this year one of the best they had ever known. A smile replaced the heavy heart, and Jonas and Jacob awoke to a cheerful mother who could not seem to stop smiling.

"Mom, what are you smiling at?" Jacob wanted to know.

"Smiling? Was I smiling?"

"You know you were. Do you have a secret?" Jonas was very sharp.

"Now you two finish your breakfast and go clean your room. Then I may have some other chores for you to do. Let's see what else I can find to keep you busy?" Maggie stopped and made a big show of propping her elbow on her hand and tapping a finger to her cheek as though she were really thinking hard.

"Jonas, don't ask anymore questions. Let's go before she can think up anymore work. We have other things to do." Jacob gave his brother a slight kick under the table as if to say, *'you know what I mean.'*

"Oh, yeah, right. We'll go clean our room now, Mom. We'll get out of your hair, Okay?"

Maggie smiled again. "Okay, scoot."

She had no way of knowing that they were making a present for her with Johnny's help. He had found an old rocking chair in a dump somewhere and had dragged it home. They had been working on it for months. They had sanded it and re-glued the seams. In some places, they had replaced parts. They only needed to paint it and put it under the tree without their mom seeing it.

Johnny knew just what to do.

"Get a big box, put a note in it that says, *'Go look on the porch,'* and wrap it. I'll bring the chair over in the middle of the night and put it on the porch. When your mom reads the note, she'll go open the door and there it will be. Surprise!" It was a great plan. So, Jonas and Jacob did just what Johnny had suggested.

Maggie, too, had made plans. She bought the crayons and books as she had planned. They were wrapped and placed under the tree on Christmas Eve. Then the three members of the Bystander family sat down together to read from the Bible about the birth of the Christ child.

"You must always remember why we have Christmas. It is because of the gift God gave to us that we give gifts to others. It is a way of showing our love for others. That is why the Bible tells us that it is more blessed to give than to receive. We bless others with our giving and in turn we are blessed ourselves."

Maggie sat curled up on the couch with the boys for a long time. Finally, she hurried them off to bed. The Reverend would be coming with the gifts before long and they needed to be asleep. The smile crept back across

Maggie's face. She could hardly wait to see their faces in the morning.

When the knock finally came at her door, Maggie's face was unforgettable. She had expected a handful of small gifts. What greeted her, however, when she opened the door was a small crowd of people with what looked like a whole store. There were sacks and sacks of packages of all shapes and sizes. There were three large boxes of food including a turkey. And at the very end of the parade of people came two boys pushing two brand new shiny boys bicycles—one blue and one green.

When she saw the bicycles, Maggie could not contain herself any longer. She covered her face and started crying. Sadie, who had been partially responsible for this surprise, came and wrapped her big arms around Maggie and patted her.

"I never expected so much!"

"This is what was left over after we finished buying everything that we could think of." Reverend Lightfoot held out an envelope filled with money. "You use it as you see fit."

Maggie cried even harder. "I don't know how to thank you all. You don't know how much this means to me." Maggie sniffed and wiped at her eyes.

Sadie hugged her again. "I don't think you know how much you mean to us, but maybe this will give you some idea."

Maggie looked at the presents stacked to overflowing under the tree and at the two bicycles. "Thank you again. Thank you so much." She shook all their hands and wished them a Merry Christmas before they left. When they were gone, she put away the food and then just sat and looked at what they had brought. She was so excited. How could she ever hope to sleep?

Surprisingly, she did sleep, and before she knew it, it was morning. Jonas and Jacob came bouncing into the room, stopped, blinked a couple of times, and then began shouting.

"Mom! Mom! Come quick and see! Mom! Mom! It must have been an angel! Come see! Mom, come see what the angels brought!"

Maggie smiled as the two excited boys tugged and pulled at her arms. They drug her into the living room before they started digging into the mountain of gifts. Maggie had moved the bicycles into the kitchen out of sight. She wanted to save them for last.

It was a long process of sorting packages and opening them one at a time. Finally, Maggie came to the one from Jonas and Jacob.

"What is this? A note?"

"Read it, Mom!" The two boys waited with expectant grins as Maggie read the note, looked at them with her suspicious eye, then went to the front door.

Johnny had not failed them. True to his word, he had left the rocking chair on the porch during the night. It was painted a dark green with little white daises laced across the headrest.

"Do you like it, Mom?"

Maggie scooped them into her arms and kissed them all over. "Like it? I love it! Almost as much as I love you two!"

"Sit in it. Try it out. It works real good."

They started pushing Maggie into the chair.

"Wait a minute!" Maggie laughed. "Let me bring it in the house first!"

Once she had it inside, she sat down and stretched out her arms. "Do you think it is big enough for three?" Without hesitation, the two boys climbed upon their mother's lap and sat there rocking with her.

"You know I almost forgot something in all the excitement."

"What's that?"

"We haven't had breakfast yet. Why don't you two hop down and go in the kitchen and wash your hands."

As they jumped off her lap and raced for the kitchen, Maggie grinned. She was not far behind them. She wanted to see their faces when they saw the bicycles. Up until that moment, she had not thought it possible for them to be so overcome with emotion that they were speechless. She was wrong.

There was no shouting. There was no jumping. Both boys stood frozen in silence with their mouths open and their eyes wide. Neither moved for what seemed like several minutes. At last, Jonas asked, "Are they ours?"

"Yes, sweetie they are yours."

Maggie was totally surprised at what happened next. Jonas and Jacob turned around and ran over to her. They threw their arms around her and started crying. "We love you, Mom."

Maggie hugged and kissed them some more before turning them loose. "I couldn't afford to buy you these things, but God knows the desires of our hearts and He knows just how and when to bless us. We are greatly loved by our neighbors."

That Christmas of 1949 was filled with many wonderful memories. They were memories that the Bystander family would always treasure.

Chapter 10

"Why can't I make the cake and you get the flowers?"

"Because I'm a better cook than you are." Jacob studied the recipe that Sadie had scratched out on a piece of paper for him.

"You go get some flowers while I mix up the cake and when it is done, we'll decorate it together. Okay?"

Satisfied with that compromise, Jonas shrugged his shoulders and nodded his agreement. "All right, I'll be back soon." ˙

Jonas shuffled out the door and headed down the road to look for flowers. Meanwhile, Jacob searched the kitchen for the bowls, pans, and ingredients necessary to make a birthday cake for their mother. He had never made a cake before, but he was not afraid to try anything. He was the daring one. Although, technically, Jonas was the oldest, Jacob was usually the leader. He rushed in at times when Jonas preferred to think about things first.

The cake was a good example. Jonas wanted to let Sadie make it, but Jacob insisted that he could do it himself. After all, he had cooked many other things, why not a cake? How hard could it be? Mother would be more surprised, and it would mean more to her if they had actually made it.

Jacob studied the instructions, measured the ingredients, and stirred the batter. Finally, he put the cake in the oven and sat down to wait for it to bake. Just as the smell of the cake began to fill the house, Jonas returned with a large collection of flowers.

"Do you think this is enough?" Jonas displayed his bundle with pride.

"Man, it looks like you picked a whole garden! Where did you find them?" Jacob studied the bouquet.

"Well, I was walking down the road not finding very much, when all of a sudden I remembered that Mrs. Snow has these huge flower beds all around her yard. I thought *'she has so many, she won't miss a few.'* So, I ran over to her house and picked a handful. She has so many that she'll never miss them."

"You mean you didn't ask her first?" Jacob was surprised.

"They're just flowers. Why would I have to ask?"

"Because, she might not want you to pick her flowers."

"I don't see why. What good are they if people can't enjoy them? I think she wants people to enjoy them, or she wouldn't have so many."

Jacob shook his head. "Well, it's too late now. I hope she doesn't get mad. Come on. Let's find something to put them in before they start to wilt."

A quick search of the kitchen produced a large fruit jar that could serve as a vase for the fragrant arrangement of flowers.

"I think the cake is just about ready." Jacob got a towel from the rack and opened the oven door. He tested the cake with a fork. It was ready. Carefully, he pulled the cake from the hot oven and placed it on top of the stove to cool.

"When do we decorate it?"

"After it cools."

"How long will that take?" Jonas looked at the clock. "It's getting late. Mom will be coming home soon."

"I know. Maybe if we put it in the window it will cool faster." Jonas ran to open the window while Jacob carefully carried the hot pan to the windowsill.

"Now…while we're waiting…we can start making the icing and get that decorating thing of Mom's ready."

"What 'decorating thing' are you talking about?"

Jacob was digging through the kitchen drawers.

"Oh, you know, that tube thing that Mom always uses to write on our cakes—the one that makes flowers and leaves. You put icing inside and then squeeze it out the tiny hole in the end."

"Oh, that thing. I know where it is." Jonas went to a cupboard and pulled out a box. "Mom likes to keep it all together in here. I guess she's afraid of losing the pieces. Some of them are pretty small."

The two boys set about making icing with powdered sugar and milk. The first batch was too thin. They had to throw it out and start over. The next batch seemed a little too thick to spread, so they added a little more milk. Finally, they agreed that it was just about right. The way Mom made hers.

They looked at the clock. It was getting late. They pulled the cake from the window and began to spread the icing. Everything seemed to be going just as they had planned. Now it was time for the decorating.

"I get to decorate. What color should we make the writing?"

Jacob looked at Jonas with a blank look on his face.

"Color?" He ran to the cupboard. "I forgot to check for coloring. I don't know if we have any."

A hasty search uncovered a box of food coloring.

"Okay, which color do we use?"

"Green."

Jacob pulled out the bottle with the green cap.

"It's empty."

"What about blue?"

Jacob pulled out the bottle with the blue lid and examined its contents. Both boys sighed with relief when they saw the bottle was not empty.

"That was close."

Jonas looked at the clock again. "Speaking of close, Mom is going to be home in about fifteen minutes, we've got to hurry."

A couple of drops of food coloring and a swift stir later, Jacob was filling the decorating tube with creamy blue icing.

"Remember, I get to do the writing."

Jacob handed over the tube.

"I'll go watch for Mother, while you finish." Jacob ran to the front window and watched the road for any sign of their mother's car.

It wasn't long before he saw her car round the corner and turn up the drive to their house.

"Jonas! She's coming!"

From the kitchen, Jonas called back. "I'm almost finished! Don't let her in yet!"

Jacob had to think fast. What could he do to stall her? Looking out the window, he saw Jonas' bicycle leaning against the porch. Quickly, he ran out the door and hopped on it. Down the lane he went. As he drew close to the end of the drive, he suddenly slid the bicycle sideways and tumbled across the grass. He rolled end over end a few times, and, when he finally stopped, he lay still and waited.

He heard the car door open and the quick footsteps of his mother as she rushed to his side.

"Jonas! Are you hurt?" Maggie turned him over and started feeling for broken bones.

Jacob moaned and groaned a bit, just for effect. "Ooooo...I...I...think I'll be okay."

"Jacob...I thought you were Jonas. What on earth were you doing?" Maggie was helping her son to his feet.

"The grass must have been a little wet and the tire slid sideways when I tried to stop." Jacob leaned on his mother's arm and kept one eye on the door of the house. He moaned some more and hobbled as slow as he could.

"Are you sure you didn't hurt something? Why were you racing down the road like that anyway?"

Jacob ignored the questions. He didn't have any answers. "I think I hit my head. Is it bleeding?" Jacob rubbed his head and wrinkled his forehead.

Margaret examined his head and looked for any sign of blood or bruising. "I don't see anything, but you had better lie down for a bit. You're not dizzy are you?"

"Dizzy?" It sounded like a good idea. Jacob staggered a little. "Things do seem to be moving some." He stumbled again just for good measure.

Margaret held his arm tighter as they continued across the yard. She was helping him up the porch steps just as Jonas appeared in the window and gave him the okay to come in.

Jacob pulled himself free of Margaret's grasp and reached for the door. "I feel much better now, Mom; I can make it by myself the rest of the way."

Margaret watched Jacob disappear through the front door of their house. Such a sudden and miraculous recovery could mean only one thing—her two boys were up to something. What could it be? The only way to find out was to open the door.

"Surprise!" Both boys shouted in unison as Margaret came through the door. They stood side-by-side grinning from ear to ear and bursting with pride. Jonas was holding the cake with 'Happy Birthday Mom' scrawled across the top in big blue letters, and Jacob was holding the fruit jar filled with flowers.

"What a wonderful surprise!" Margaret took the flowers from Jacob, smelled them and gave him a kiss on the cheek.

"We made the cake all by ourselves."

"You did?" Margaret gave Jonas a kiss on the cheek, too.

"Well, Jacob made the cake but I helped with the icing and did the writing."

"It looks great and I bet it tastes great, too."

Jacob started pushing Margaret toward the kitchen. "We need to put the candles on top so you can make a wish and blow them out. Then we can have a piece."

Jonas set the cake on the table and started putting candles on it. Margaret set the flowers in the window and pulled out a chair. She looked around the kitchen and took note of the mess the two ten-year-old boys had made in their first attempt at baking. She smiled to herself. What would those two think of next?

"Okay, Mom, make a wish and blow out the candles."

"There are so many; I don't know if I can, but I'll try." Margaret closed her eyes…paused…then took a deep breath and blew out the candles. It was lucky for her that she didn't have enough candles to match her age.

"We have a present for you, too." Jacob ran out of the room. When he returned a few seconds later, he held a blue piece of paper rolled up like a scroll, and tied with a white ribbon.

"Open it!"

Margaret slid the ribbon off the end and started to unroll the paper. They had used crayon to trace the outline of their feet and hands down the length of the paper. Their names were written inside each handprint and footprint. On the end, they had drawn a heart with an arrow through it and written the words 'We love you, Mom.'

Margaret beamed with pride and her eyes began to water a little. "This is so thoughtful. I shall treasure it always." Her words were soft and tender.

"Do you really like it?" Jonas wanted to know.

"Like it? I love it. The only things I love more are the originals. Come here you two and let me kiss you." Margaret held out her arms. Having grown too big to sit on Mom's lap, and almost as tall as she, they took turns leaning over her as she hugged and kissed them.

"Now, where is a knife so we can cut the cake?"

Jonas produced a knife and Jacob pulled out the plates and forks. No one cared about the mess in the kitchen or that they were having desert before dinner. For Jonas and Jacob, it had been a successful surprise. For Margaret, it had been a perfect birthday.

Chapter 11

Margaret sat in her car and studied her home of fifteen years. It was so full of memories—every board, every window, and every crack in the paint held pieces of her past. It was the only home that she and Will had shared together.

He had brought her here as a new bride in 1940. He had carried her up those steps and through that very door. She could still remember the touch of his strong arms around her. She closed her eyes and tried to hear the sound of his voice. What would he say if he were here? Would he agree with her decision?

Margaret opened her eyes. Will wasn't here and he couldn't help her. It would not change circumstances to dream about impossibilities. She looked again at the front door of her home. So much of her life had passed through that door-the telegram that told of Will's death, the package bearing the watch and letter from Reverend Lansing, and the box containing the urn filled with his ashes. Her two boys were born just beyond it. She had held their hands as they walked through it and down the steps on their first day of school. She remembered the parade of people carrying Christmas presents as they marched beneath its mantle, the rocking chair it had concealed, the first birthday cake they made for her, and all the other surprises that had followed.

Memories were everywhere. Jonas and Jacob had learned to walk in this yard. They had helped her plant the flowers that grew by the porch. She had spent hours watching them ride their tricycle up and down the drive; later, she had watched them as they raced on their bicycles.

A flood of images from the past swept past her mind in only a few minutes.

Margaret opened the car door and started toward the house. She walked slower than usual. On the top step, she paused to study the lines that notched the post on either side marking the growth of her sons. Her finger traced first one then the other. On the right was Jonas. On the left was Jacob. Thirteen lines on each showed how much they had grown. Where had her babies gone? They were taller than she was and still growing.

The door suddenly opened and startled Margaret back into the present.

"Mom, what are you doin' just standin' there on the porch? Aren't you hungry? I know I am." Jacob started pulling at his mother's arm. "Jonas and me went fishin' with Johnny today and did we ever catch a mess of fish! They're out back finishin' up on the cleanin' and Sadie has got everything ready in the kitchen for a fish fry. Ain't it grand!"

"Isn't it grand, and yes it is." Margaret and Sadie exchanged looks. They knew what other surprise the evening would hold.

"I had some cornbread baking; so, I just brought it over, and I had the boys pick some tomatoes out of the garden. I hope you don't mind."

Margaret patted Sadie on the shoulder as she walked over to look out the kitchen window. She watched the two fishermen in back, as they worked steadily at the task of cleaning their catch. Meanwhile, Jacob never ceased or paused for breath in his long narrative of their day. He wanted to describe in great detail the battle for each and every fish.

Margaret turned to her son. "Why aren't you helping them clean?"

"I did help some." He turned to Sadie.

"Didn't I Sadie? You saw me."

"That's true; he was cleaning fish when I got here."

"And?"

"And then we decided since I'm the best cook, and I'm going to help with the cooking, that I shouldn't have to clean them too."

Margaret nodded her head. "I see." She looked out the window again before pulling out a chair and sitting down at the table with Sadie. "Since you're going to do part of the cooking, and you're starving, I suggest you get started while I rest for a few minutes. But before you begin, how about a glass of water and a kiss?"

Jacob filled a glass and set it down in front of his mother. As he started to back away, she turned her head slightly to one side and tapped her cheek with one finger.

"Ah, Mom, we have company." He whined.

Margaret tapped her check again. Reluctantly and very quickly, Jacob gave her a quick peck on the check. Sadie turned her head slightly and hid a faint grin behind her hand.

"Now, that didn't hurt, did it? Run outside and see if they are about finished, so we can get started with this fish fry."

Jacob didn't have to be told twice. He was out the door and gone practically before Margaret had finished her sentence. Gone with him were the smiles and light-heartedness that had only a few moments before filled the tiny kitchen. In their place, came an air of heaviness and a sense of mourning.

"Are you going to tell them tonight?"

"Yes."

"Do you want me to stay?"

"Have you told Johnny, yet?"

"No, I'm as big a coward as you are. I just kept hoping that something would change."

"I know; I did, too. Unfortunately, it hasn't, and I can't wait any longer. Things just keep getting worse. I need you to stay and help me, Sadie. We can tell them all at the same time. Maybe it will be easier that way—for all of us."

"I don't think anything will make it easier, but I'll stay."

Margaret reached across the table and squeezed Sadie's hand. "What would I have done without you all these years? You've been a friend and a mother to me."

Sadie's lower lip began to quiver a little. "And you've been like a daughter to me, and"—she nodded in the direction of the back yard—"those boys have been the closest things to grandchildren I think I'll ever have."

About that time, all three sons came charging into the kitchen carrying a big pan of fish ready for frying. Sadie and Margaret quickly hid their sad faces behind a veil of smiles. Jonas plopped his pan down in front of Margaret, leaned over, and gave her a hasty kiss on the cheek.

"Hi, Mom. Guess who caught the biggest fish?" Without waiting for her to reply, he answered his own question. "Me!" He stretched his arms out to emphasis the size. "It was this big!"

Jacob and Johnny were grinning from ear to ear. Johnny leaned over the table and whispered softly. "Ask him what happened to it."

Margaret watched Jonas squirm a little. "It wasn't my fault the fish was too heavy for the line. My line broke before I could get it in the boat and it got away."

The entire room burst into a round of laughter. Jonas laughed right along with them. He liked a good fish story as well as the next person.

The two families set about to make this evening as enjoyable as possible. They laughed and told stories while they were cooking. The boys, who needed very little encouragement to recount their many adventures, told story after story. Several times, all three of them tried to talk at once. At other times, one would start a tale, another would pick it up at mid-point, and the third would finish it.

While Sadie, Margaret, and Jacob prepared the food, the other two kept them entertained. During dinner, the evening grew quieter, but only because they liked to eat just about as much as they liked to talk.

It was a very pleasant time for all.

The evening was quickly slipping away as Margaret rose from the table. "I think I shall leave you boys to your tall tales and start cleaning this kitchen."

Sadie collected the empty plates near her and followed Margaret to the sink. They worked together in silence, while only a few feet away, their sons chattered on and on without realizing the change that was about to descend upon them.

"Why don't you boys go in the other room and let us finish in here."

They needed no additional instructions. A hasty escape would guarantee no dishes to wash, dry, or put away. Jacob led the charge for the living room with Jonas close behind.

Johnny knew from years of experience not to get in their path when they were racing.

In what seemed like only a few minutes, Sadie and Margaret had finished the dishes and prepared to join their boys. Neither woman was looking forward to what was going to happen next. This was one time Margaret would have welcomed more dishes to wash, but there were none. They exchanged silent words of encouragement—each woman understanding the thoughts of the other. Dread filled their hearts with heaviness and made their limbs feel like lead. Slowly, they went to face the moment of truth.

They emerged from the kitchen unnoticed by the three boys. Sadie found a chair and sat with her hands folded. Maggie stood with her hands nervously twisting a towel she had used to dry her hands. She had been absent minded to carry it away with her, but was now thankful for it. Jonas and Jacob were lying on the floor with their arms braced for another round of arm wrestling.

Margaret cleared her throat. "Boys, I need you to stop for a moment. I need to talk with you about something important."

Jacob called from the floor without taking his eyes off his brother, "Give me just a minute, Mom, that's all I need to beat Jonas."

"You wish!"

"Now, please."

They reluctantly dropped their arms and twisted into a sitting position without further argument.

"Lucky for you. I was getting ready to beat you.

Jonas punched Jacob playfully in the shoulder. "Not a chance."

"As you know, business has been slow and I was let go some weeks ago. I've been trying to find work here, but business is bad for everyone it seems. Things have been very tight. We have managed to eat well enough with the garden, and the fish that you have caught...You have worked very hard mowing yards and doing other odd jobs to help pay the bills—and I appreciate it more than you know—but we can't go on this way." Margaret paused for a minute to compose herself before continuing. "I wanted so much for things to be different, but they aren't. The only thing I can do now is go where the jobs are." She waited for a reaction. None came. "We will have to move to Tulsa, and we will have to move before school starts."

"No! Mom! No! You'll find something here if you just keep looking." Jonas pleaded.

"We'll work harder!" Jacob turned to Jonas for support. "Won't we, Jonas? We'll help more! We'll get jobs!"

Margaret shook her head. "It won't work, and I can't let you carry so much responsibility. If we were to stay here, winter would find us easy prey. This was a hard decision. I didn't make it lightly. I know what you will have to leave behind." Margaret's voice cracked, her eyes watered, and her lip quivered, "I know."

The two boys looked at Sadie in disbelief. She was wiping her eyes. Then they looked at Johnny. He sat with a face of stone, too grief stricken to speak.

"No! I won't go! It's not fair to ask us to leave Sadie and Johnny!" Jacob jumped to his feet.

Jonas hesitated a second or two, and then joined him. "Mom, you can't do this! You can't take us away from everyone and everything we love." He looked at his mother with pleading eyes.

67

"Don't you think I know how hard this will be?" Margaret's voice was strained.

"No! No! I don't, or you wouldn't even suggest it!" Jacob began stomping around in circles.

"Well, I do know." Tears began to trickle down Margaret's cheeks—the same cheeks that only a short time before her boys had kissed with loving tenderness. "I have to leave everyone and everything I hold dear, too. Everything, that is, except you two."

"But we can help." Jonas pleaded again.

Margaret only shook her head.

"Try harder. Maybe you can still find work here? There must be something?"

"I have tried. Really, I have. This was a very hard decision and I thought it over very carefully. There aren't any other options."

Johnny had sat silently listening. When he spoke, he sounded calm. "How far is Tulsa?"

"About ninety or a hundred miles."

Johnny thought for a moment. "Is there an ocean between here and there?"

"No, no ocean."

Johnny looked at Jonas and Jacob with a very serious expression. The wheels in his head could almost be seen turning. "I crossed an ocean. I walked all over Europe for two years. I know it was more than a hundred miles. I left everyone and everything I loved. It was hard, but I had to go. It wasn't forever. I've been home now for longer than I was gone." He shook his head and moved to hug the boys and pat them on their backs. "A hundred miles is nothing to us. I bet we've walked that and then some this summer fishing and hunting."

"I guess that's true."

"You know it is. So, straighten up and do what's right," Johnny shook his head again, "and not what's easy."

Sadie was very proud of her son at that moment. He talked as though he were normal again.

"Mom, I think we should go now."

Sadie agreed. "Maggie, I'll talk to you tomorrow. Thanks for dinner."

"Good night. Thanks for your support."

Sadie and Johnny left the Bystander family alone to work out their future. It would be a future without the everyday supervision of Johnny. This was a fact that was painfully apparent to him. His brief moment of strength and normalcy gave way to self-indulgence as he allowed himself to cry once they were outside. He turned to Sadie and she held him as he cried on her shoulder.

"Mom, what am I going to do without them? They are like my own."

Sadie didn't have an answer. Her own heart was breaking under the weight of the same question. "What am I going to do without them?"

Chapter 12

The next couple of weeks were filled with activity. Margaret traveled to Tulsa in search of a job. Jonas and Jacob spent as much time as possible with Johnny. They practically lived in the woods. They would camp by the lake or by a river, and stay awake most of the night talking. They talked about things they had done and things they were going to do.

On one of these nights, Johnny had an idea that everyone agreed was spectacular.

"Let's make a teepee like the one Reverend Lightfoot has, and on the outside we can paint pictures of our adventures just the way our people used to do. When we go camping, we can take it with us and use it for shelter. In the summer, when you are out of school, we can live in it for as long as your mother will let us."

The idea caught their imaginations like wild fire. So much so, that they hardly slept at all that night. The dawn was too slow in coming. When it finally arrived, the three companions set about the task of making a teepee.

They worked as they had never worked before. Their singleness of mind was uncanny. They barely spoke at times. It was almost as if they could read each other's thoughts.

They cut twelve long poles then stripped them of their bark. That was the easy part. Next, they had to find enough canvas to cover the poles, which would form the walls. Traditionally, they were supposed to use animal skins or buffalo hides, but, since they didn't have either, canvas would have to do. They asked everyone they knew for old tents, army cots, or tarps. Eventually, they had enough. It was a pretty comical sight when they were finished. It looked more like a patchwork quilt than a teepee; however, they thought it was perfect.

The only thing left to do was the painting of scenes on the outside. They sketched out on paper their ideas. It was hard to decide which ones to draw because they had done so much in their years together. Finally, Jonas had an idea. Each section would contain an event for each year Johnny had been with them.

In one scene, Johnny was carrying one boy on his shoulders and holding the other by the hand as they walked through the woods picking black berries. In another, Johnny was teaching them to swim. It showed them swinging from a rope that hung over the water. Yet, another showed Johnny teaching them to shoot and hunt. There was a string of fish hanging over a campfire, and a deer tied by its feet hung on a pole suspended on the shoulders of the two boys. Always, the three were together; always, they would be together in heart and soul.

The final touches completed, the three friends stood back to admire their handiwork. Gone was the patchwork quilt; in its place was a work of art. They stood silent and studied the overall picture. It was as if their lives were passing before their eyes and they were amazed at how much they had done and shared.

Johnny was the first to speak. "Well, boys, I think she's ready."

Jacob made a dash for the opening. "Last one in is a rotten egg!" He lunged for the flap that covered the entrance.

Jonas was close on his heels and Johnny came last. Once inside, they laughed and stretched out on the floor to get the feel of it.

"Let's sleep in here tonight."

"Think Mom will let us?"

"Sure, why not?"

"When she gets back tonight I'll ask; meanwhile, what do you say we go fishin'." Johnny had been lying stretched out with his hands under his head. He rolled over on his side and propped himself up on one elbow. "Smoked fish over a camp fire sure sounds good to me. How 'bout you?"

Jonas and Jacob needed no encouragement. They were up and running for their poles practically before Johnny had finished talking. Within ten minutes, the three were winding their way down the trails and slopes toward their favorite fishing hole.

They sat with bare feet hanging over the water quietly baiting their hooks. Each time someone got a bite, the others would shout words of encouragement or instructions if necessary. They didn't care who had the biggest fish or who had caught the most. They were a team. As the day began to wind down and the sun dropped below the treetops, Johnny announced that it was time to go home.

"We best be headin' for home."

"Oh, just a little longer."

"The fish are really biting good."

"We have enough fish, and your mother is probably home now and she'll be worried." Johnny started preparing to leave. He pulled the days catch up out of the water and counted the fish.

"…seven, eight, nine, ten."

"Come on, Jacob. We have enough." Jonas reeled in his line and prepared to leave.

"Oh, okay. I guess you're right." Reluctantly, Jacob followed Jonas' example and prepared to leave.

On the way back, they took turns carrying the fish and discussed how they were going to cook them. They had visions of an open campfire with their afternoon catch dangling over the smoke and flames. Johnny looked at the sky as they drew near to home.

"I don't know boys. The sky is getting awfully dark. We may have rain before we can get a fire going."

It was true. The sky was growing dark and not just from the setting sun.

"What's a little rain? We'll make our camp fire inside the teepee just the way our ancestors did." Jacob was not going to be intimidated by a few clouds.

"Don't forget, Jacob, we still have to ask Mom. She may have a different idea." Jonas studied the clouds. "I'm not so sure that it's only going to be a 'little' rain."

About that time, they caught sight of their house through the trees and on the porch stood their mother. She appeared to be looking for them. She had one hand on her hip and the other shading her eyes as she searched the surrounding terrain. Almost simultaneously, the two brothers broke into a run and took off with shouts of greeting toward their mother.

Margaret heard them and hurried to meet them with open arms. She hugged first one then the other before kissing both of them on the cheek.

"Boy, have I missed you two!"

"We missed you, too, Mom."

Margaret nodded in the direction of the teepee. "I can tell. It appears as though you did find a way to occupy yourselves."

Jacob started tugging at Margaret's arm. "It was Johnny's idea! How do you like it?"

Johnny added, "We just finished it today."

Margaret walked around the teepee and studied the pictures. "You put a lot of work into this. I'm impressed."

Jonas held the flap open for Margaret to enter. "There's lots of room inside. Three people could easily stretch out and sleep in here."

Margaret looked at Jonas as she ducked under the flap and surveyed the interior.

"Yes, I see it's very roomy." Margaret stood in the middle and looked around. "It would be a shame to build something so special and not use it. How would you like to sleep out here tonight?"

Margaret watched as the three tried to act as though the idea had not occurred to them. She knew them too well. From the first moment she had driven up the road and seen the teepee, she had known that they would want to sleep in it—if they hadn't already. Who would put so much work into something and then not use it?

"Can we cook our fish out here, too?" Jonas held up the string of fish.

Margaret gave a sideways glance at Johnny before answering. His eyes meet hers and there was a silent conversation exchanged between them in those few seconds. Johnny's eyes assured her that he would be present to supervise and protect her two sons.

"Okay."

Shouts of joy erupted from the two youths.

"On one condition," Jonas and Jacob waited. "That you let me join you for dinner. I haven't had any good fish for a long time."

"It's a deal!" They all answered together.

"Of course, Mom. We wouldn't leave you out. Come on, Jacob, let's go get some rocks and fire wood." With that, the two boys ran out the door and left Margaret and Johnny alone.

"Don't worry, Maggie. I'll keep a close eye on them. They'll be safe."

Margaret patted Johnny on the shoulder. "I know you will. I really appreciate how you have watched over them all these years. I feel really bad for moving them away."

Sensing that there was more to what she said, Johnny asked, "Are you taking them back with you this time?"

"Yes, I've got a place for us to live, and school will be starting in another week. I have to get them situated." Margaret watched Johnny's face grow sad.

"I understand."

They walked outside in silence. Margaret stopped to study the darkening sky. Her brow wrinkled with concern.

"I hope this is a good idea. I don't like the looks of those clouds." She looked back at Johnny. He was studying them, too. She wondered what thoughts were going through his mind just then. Sadie had shared with her how he reacted to storms. "Are you sure you can do this? There will be other days?"

Johnny pressed his teeth tightly together and set his jaw in a determined manner. It was as if he were defying the heavens to rob him and his two friends of this special night.

"I won't let them down…I can't."

Margaret could see the determination in his face and nodded her understanding. About that time, Jonas and Jacob came charging through the yard with their arms full of wood.

"Don't forget the stones!" Johnny looked at the sky. "It looks like rain, so we'll cook inside."

"That's okay with us. It will be even more fun that way."

Johnny stooped to pick up the string of fish, which still lay where it had been dropped. "I'll just take care of this little chore while you two get the fire ready." With that, Johnny headed to the back of the house with the fish. The brothers scurried about collecting rocks as flat as possible for the fire.

Margaret sat contentedly watching from the rocker on the porch. She wanted to engrave this scene on her memory for the future. In the years ahead when they were far from the Seneca hills, her memories would be all that were left of this happy time. As the shadows grew long and the light faded, she mentally began to say her good-byes to all that had been and to turn her face toward what would be the start of a new day and a new life.

Chapter 13

A circle of stones contained the small fire in the center of the room. The slender pillar of smoke ascended straight up and out the narrow opening at the top of the teepee where the poles were tied together. The steady rain that had begun to fall could be heard as it hit the canvas and was amplified. All else inside was quiet.

Jonas and Jacob were asleep. They were peacefully unaware of any problem, as they lay curled up on their blankets. To them, it was only a little rain, nothing to lose sleep over. If anything, the rain only made their campout more of an adventure. They didn't know that rain and storms opened a nightmare world for Johnny. He had never told them.

He had never been able to share with them what he tried so desperately to forget. He prayed he could make it through the night. He had nervously watched the clouds gather and had desperately wanted to escape to the safety of his own four walls. However, he had found himself unable to disappoint his two best friends. Now he lay frozen in the darkness with fear. He struggled with all his might to control the panic.

Low rumbles of thunder in the distance caused him to start shaking. He clinched his teeth tight together and squeezed his eyes shut. When he opened them, he saw a faint flash of lightning and another roll of thunder followed. The storm was coming closer and growing louder. He sat up, clasped his hands over his ears, and squeezed his eyes as tight as he could. His body began to shake even harder as he struggled to control the scream that threatened to escape his throat. Remember! He must remember Jonas and Jacob.

The thunder came again closer and louder. His hands could not block the sound. A quivering moan escaped his lips but the two sleeping boys were undisturbed. At that moment, a bolt of lightening struck so close that it sounded as though a bomb had exploded next to them. This time Johnny could not contain the scream, but it was lost in the echo of the blast, and neither boy heard it. Instead, they were shaken from their sleep by the force of the lightening strike and were on their feet in seconds.

"What was that!"

"It was really close! I wonder where it hit!"

"Johnny, where do you think it hit?"

There was no answer.

"Johnny?"

For the first time, the two young boys looked in the direction of their friend. What they saw was a small shape huddled up against the canvas wall. They took a cautious step toward him.

"Johnny?"

The shape began to moan and sob as it rocked back and forth. His arms moved between hugging his legs and pressing his hands against his ears in an attempt to block out the noise.

"Johnny? What's wrong?" The two boys forgot about the storm and inched closer.

Johnny's voice came in low pleading whimpers. "Stop, please make them stop."

"It's just rain and thunder, Johnny. We can't make it stop."

"I don't want to see any more death. I can't stand to lose any more friends. Please, no more killing."

Now Jonas and Jacob were on either side of him. They tried to comfort him and assure him that no one was going to die. The war had been over for a long time, and the noise was only thunder not bombs. Johnny didn't seem to hear or understand. He just kept pleading for the bombs to stop. Suddenly, he grew quiet. His eyes were fixed in a glassy stare. The boys looked at each other bewildered by his sudden silence. They watched as the look on his face slowly began to change to one of terror. Without warning, Johnny jumped to his feet and screamed. He darted out the covered entrance and left the two brothers sitting alone and wondering what had happened.

They didn't wonder long. A faint glow of light and moving shadows on the teepee wall soon caught their attention.

"Jacob, look!"

They both watched in disbelief, as the light grew brighter. It could mean only one thing. Quickly, they scrambled outside and looked in the direction of their home. It was on fire. The lightning bolt that they had heard had struck their house.

Johnny was running back and forth across the yard screaming at the sky to stop. He stopped and dropped to his knees, pressed his hands over his ears as hard as he could, and bent his head until it touched the rain soaked ground.

"Please, please stop!" He begged through his tears.

Jonas and Jacob only had a moment to observe Johnny before they turned their attention to the burning house.

"Mom! Where's Mom!"

"She must still be inside!" Even before Jacob had finished speaking, both boys had begun running and in only a few seconds were on the porch and through the door.

It was dark and smoky inside, but they didn't need to see to know the way. Fourteen years had taught them the exact number of steps from door to door and every turn between.

The blast had shaken Margaret from her bed. She lay stunned on the floor and stared blankly at the ceiling. What had happened? She tried to remember. The room seemed to move as fingers of light danced on the walls. What was that smell? What was that sound? Slowly, her mind began to clear and Margaret knew. It was smoke and the snap and crackle of burning wood.

Margaret tried to move but her arms and legs felt like lead. She turned her head and the room began to swim. She closed her eyes again and murmured a quick prayer. She opened her eyes and commanded her body to move. Carefully, she rolled over on her side, then her stomach. Gathering her strength, Margaret began to crawl toward the door. She had only gone a few inches when she felt strong hands and arms lifting her off the floor.

"Jonas? Jacob?"

"We have you, Mom."

The two boys, with their mother between them, stumbled coughing and choking through the front door. Once outside, they paused to catch a breath of clean air before continuing down the steps and into the rain. Behind them the fire was spreading and was slowly swallowing everything they owned.

Jacob let go of his mother's arm as he shouted over his shoulder. "I'm going back for the chest!"

"Jacob, no!" Margaret grabbed for his arm, but she was too late.

Jonas quickly pulled his mother off the porch and out of harms way. "Wait here! I'll help him!"

Jonas raced back into the burning house and retraced the steps that he and Jacob had taken only seconds before. Even in those few seconds the atmosphere inside the cabin had changed. The smoke was thicker and it stung his eyes. The heat from the flames was almost unbearable.

Outside, alone in the rain, Margaret fell on her knees and began to pray as she had never prayed before. She prayed for God to send a miracle for her boys...and He did. The miracle was Johnny.

Johnny had not moved from the spot where he had first dropped to his knees. He had watched in horror as his two young friends had gone into the burning house and emerged with their mother unharmed. Then he watched as they ran—first one then the other—back into the house to retrieve the chest containing the memories of their father. He waited...They were taking too long.

"No..." It was a whisper under his breath. "No..." He spoke the word louder. "NO!" He shouted in anger at an unseen, uncaring enemy. Leaping to his feet, Johnny ran shouting onto the porch, "Not this time! Not this time!" and disappeared into the house.

Three miles away, Sadie had watched the dark clouds roll across the horizon all afternoon. Would it be just rain or would it be a thunderstorm? She nervously checked and rechecked the progress of the clouds. She had not been too concerned when Johnny had first told her that he and the boys were going to spend this last night in their teepee. It was important to them. Tomorrow, they would be leaving for Tulsa, and God only knew how long it would be before they would see each other again.

Had she known earlier about the possibility of a storm, she would have protested. She knew from past experience what effect storms had on Johnny. Many times she had left her bed when the thunder started and found him huddled in a corner. His knees drawn up under his chin and his hands clasped over his ears. He would scream at the storm to stop, and then shake uncontrollably. She would hold him and try to calm him, but he never really seemed to know she was there.

Sadie paced the floor and wiped her hands nervously on a towel. What would he do if he were alone with the boys during a thunderstorm? What if he forgot where he was and didn't know who they were? What if he thought they were the unseen enemy of his nightmares? Sadie had never shared this side of Johnny with anyone except Maggie. It was a carefully guarded secret.

She looked out the window again. The clouds continued to blanket the sky and the day grew dark earlier than usual. *'What should I do?'* she wondered. A stirring inside told Sadie to pray and so she did. She found her Bible and sat in the middle of Johnny's bed. She lifted her voice to heaven and began to pray.

There she sat. At times she would stop and read her Bible. Then she would begin talking to God again. In the midst of this, the rain began to fall. The thunder and lightning filled the night. The hours passed, and Sadie grew tired but found she could not sleep; a growing sense of foreboding wouldn't let her.

Shortly after midnight, Sadie heard lightning strike close by. She ran to a window and looked in the direction of

Maggie's house. She stood frozen...waiting. A faint glow seemed to hover over the top of the trees. At first, she wasn't sure if it was her imagination or reality. She watched as the glow became brighter and brighter until there was no doubt. There was a fire and it was in the direction of Maggie's house.

There was no time to waste. Sadie flew from the window, out the front door, and jumped into her car. The normal drive on the winding roads to Maggie's house only took eight minutes, but, on this night, it seemed an eternity. With each passing mile, Sadie could see the flames growing brighter and reaching above the trees. She struggled to control her fear and panic. Her imagination threatened to overrun her and consume her.

"Oh, God...Oh, God...let them all be safe." Sadie whispered the words under her breath as she sped through the darkness. She was overcome by what she saw when she rounded the last curve and raced up the drive toward the house. Her hands gripped the steering wheel until her knuckles turned white. She leaned forward as though, somehow, it would get her there faster. Her heart raced and her nerves tensed.

Maggie was sitting on the ground in the rain with a blanket around her. One of the boys was dragging a trunk out the door while flames were shooting from the roof. Sadie caught her breath again. "Oh, God!" Where were Johnny and the other boy?

She brought the car to a sudden stop and raced to Maggie's side. As she drew near she could see that it was Jacob who struggle with the chest.

"Where are Johnny and Jonas?"

Jacob sank to one knee coughing. When he recovered, he shouted over the roar of the fire. "He was right behind me! He was helping Jonas!" Jacob looked up. The light of the fire reflected off his face smudged with soot and smoke. "Oh, God! He was right behind me!" Fear and anguish vibrated in his voice.

Sadie put her arms around Jonas to steady him. The three stood frozen like statues in the rain. Clinging to each other, they waited...The flames were swallowing the small house board by board. They listened to the house moan as it slowly succumbed to the flames.

Margaret couldn't look any longer. She turned her face and buried her head in Sadie's bosom. But Sadie had to watch; her life was in that house. She fixed her eyes on what had been the front door and willed her son to appear through the flames.

Jacob had risen to his feet and was standing firm and straight with clenched fists. Sadie could see his jaw set and rigid with determination, as he silently dared the fire to take his brother and friend. They waited, suspended between heaven and earth.

Suddenly, the spell was broken as a tremendous crashing sound filled the air. Flames and smoke shot high into the air and out the windows. The sound was so sudden and loud that Margaret started and turned just in time to see Johnny emerge from the flames with Jonas slung over his shoulders like a sack of potatoes. He ran with feet that didn't even appear to touch the ground while the fire licked at his heels.

Just beyond the reach of the crashing walls, Johnny collapsed. Jonas tumbled onto the ground coughing and choking. Sadie raced to help her son, while Margaret and

Jacob went to the aid of the rescued brother. No one seemed to notice or care about the rain.

"What happened to you? You were right behind me? You were holding the other end of the chest?"

Jonas spoke between coughs. "I tripped...over something and...lost my hold...then...I couldn't find...you."

Margaret wrapped her blanket around his shoulders and began to wipe his face with a torn piece of her gown. "I am so thankful to God that you are both okay." Her voice cracked as she realized how close she had come to loosing her two boys. She looked first at one then the other with tears in her eyes. She hugged them both as hard as she could. When she finally released them, she turned her attention to Sadie and Johnny.

"Johnny...thank you doesn't seem to be enough, but...thank you."

Johnny sat quietly with his arm around his mother. For the first time since he had left for Europe, he was not afraid. The demons that had plagued his dreams were gone. He looked at the dying house and felt only peace.

Jonas was the first to ask the question that was on everyone's mind. "Johnny, what happened to you?"

Johnny looked first at his mother then off into the distant past. "The war was very terrible. There were bombs dropping all the time, huge guns blasting at all hours of the night and day—death and destruction everywhere. It was best never to make friends because it was too painful to lose them. Never the less, I did make one friend, Pete. We watched out for each other. We went through many battles together.

One day we entered this little town. It was deserted and in ruins because of heavy bombing. We thought it would be nice to sleep under a roof for a change. We were tired of the mud and the cold. We found a cozy spot and settled in for the night...us and a couple of other guys. We drew straws to see who would take the first watch. Someone always had to be on watch, especially in a town. Well, it was me.

Things were fairly quiet at first, but then, without warning, the shelling started. The house took a direct hit—the house where my best friend was sleeping. The blast knocked me about fifteen feet. I was stunned for a few minutes. When I recovered, I could see the house engulfed in flames. I tried to get them out, but I couldn't get through the fire." Johnny looked at his mother again. "I always thought I should have been able to get them out. I felt guilty that I was spared and not Pete. He left behind a wife and a daughter."

No one spoke. The only sounds were those of the crackling fire and the lingering rumbles of distant thunder. Even the rain had become gentler. Johnny wrapped both arms around his mother as she buried her face in his chest. She would not have been able to contain the flood of tears that streamed down her face even if she had wished to. Her son had finally come home.

Chapter 14

A strange stillness settled over the room as Margaret paused in her story. A cloud of sorrow seemed to hang in the air and Margaret's shoulders drooped with an unseen weight. She looked much older to me now than when we had first sat down in the floor with the chest between us. Gone was the bounce and excitement that had filled her every word as she talked of her husband and her children.

Margaret took a deep breath and sighed as she brushed away a tear.

"We lost Sadie to cancer about two years later. Johnny...well...after Sadie died, he moved to California. He had begun communicating with the family of the friend he had lost in the war and eventually married his friend's widow. We kept in touch with Johnny by mail for a long time, but time and distance can be very cruel. He wasn't their playmate anymore. Everything had changed. Even though Jacob and Jonas never forgot Johnny, and Johnny had a special place in his heart for them, things were never the same again."

Margaret paused again to reflect. I assumed she was racing over the years and deciding what to tell me next, so I waited patiently until she was ready to continue. When she finally broke the silence, her voice was barely audible and I wondered if she even remembered I was in the room.

"I have often wondered how things might have turned out if I had stayed in Seneca. Strange how one decision can change the course of so many lives...I thought I was making the only choice available to me. I thought it was the best choice, but..." She shook her head slightly. "Now I'm not so sure."

I didn't know what to say. Presently, she continued.

"So many things changed when we moved to Tulsa, some were good and some were not. I have asked myself over and over if I did the right thing." Margaret raised her eyes to meet mine. "And the answer is always the same. I might have changed my mind and stayed in Seneca if it had not been for the fire. The fire destroyed the anchor that could have held me there. In the end...I had no other choice but to go. I have to believe that it was all part of God's plan."

'God's plan? Plan for what?' I was afraid to ask.

"Life in Tulsa was different. The bond between the boys grew even stronger. I hadn't thought it possible. They were inseparable. Oh, what trouble those two could get into." Margaret's voice held a slight chuckle as she shook her head. "What one couldn't think of to do, the other one did."

"Just imagine my horror when I returned home from work one day to find that they had 'scalped' the neighbor's dog!" Margaret laughed at the memory.

"Scalped?" I asked.

Margaret patted my hand as she explained. "They didn't kill the dog. They just shaved the hair off the top of its head. My neighbor was very mad. I had to scold them and make them apologize, but I have to admit it was funny." Margaret laughed again. "It was the most annoying dog. It was always barking in the middle of the night with its high-pitched squeaky bark that made the hair on the back of my neck stand on end. That dog looked so funny that I had a hard time keeping a straight face when I saw it. The hair grew back in a few weeks, but, from then on, anytime that dog started barking, the boys would run for the clippers. They would go to the window and turn them on. As soon as that dog heard the buzzing sound, he would shut up and run for cover."

I asked between the laughter. "Why did they do it?"

"Apparently, they were sitting around talking with friends when the topic of scalping came up. One thing led to another until one of the boys came up with the idea of the dog. They shouldn't have done it, and perhaps I didn't punish them as severely as I should have, but I did the best I could and prayed it was enough."

Margaret sighed and wrinkled her eyebrows a bit.

"They gave their teachers a hard time, too, and me nightmares. I prayed for them all the time. It's a good thing that I did, too, because...well, who can say where they would have ended without God's protection. I'm not saying my prayers are special, but God hears our prayers and it is through them that miracles happen."

I squirmed a bit at the mention of prayers. I had heard plenty on that subject, and wasn't too sure I wanted to hear more. Thankfully, Margaret did not pursue it.

"Their first years here were hard. They made poor choices in friends, but, in spite of their wild years in school, they did manage to graduate. No one could have been more surprised than they were...unless it was their teachers. They had certainly not worked at graduating; never the less, they did."

"After graduating, they drifted without direction or goals, and the associations that they had formed in high school followed them. They ran with a wild bunch of boys...not a street gang like the ones in New York or L.A...just a tight knit group of outcasts who met in school and stuck together. Willie, Tom, Rob, and Nick were their names. They had been together since grade school—my boys were the new kids. Jacob and Jonas needed to belong somewhere and that particular group accepted them as they were."

Margaret went on to explain.

"They saw city life as too confining and assumed they would never fit in. I watched as different ones from church tried to welcome them and include them in activities, but they wouldn't respond."

She turned to me with a question.

"Do you have any idea what it is like to watch your children slowly slip away? To watch them making choices that will eventually ruin their lives? I could see what was happening, but couldn't seem to find a way to stop it. I felt so helpless."

"Why do you think it was so hard for them?"

Margaret began tenderly to return items to the chest. The sparkle and energy that had radiated from her were gone. "I don't really know. I spent as much time with them as I could. I tried to get them involved in youth activities at church. I tried everything I could think of to help them…but nothing seemed to work."

I thought now was perhaps a good time to ask a question that had been nagging at me. "Didn't you ever think of remarrying? It must have been very lonely for you; you were so young."

Margaret closed the lid on the box of memories. She brushed her hand across the roughly carved letters on the surface as she considered my question. Her eyes wandered off into space before finally returning to meet mine.

"At first, I didn't think about it. How could I? I was so busy trying to take care of my boys...and then there was the war. Most of the available men were gone. It was years before I could even think of anyone but Will. When I did begin to think that I would like to remarry...I just never found anyone who could replace him in my heart. I didn't sit down one day and say to myself, *'I'm never going to get married again.'* It just turned out that way..." Margaret shrugged her shoulders and shook her head. "Time just slipped away. I woke up one day and twenty years had gone by...then thirty...then forty. Have I been lonely? Of course, I have, but even married people can be lonely. I have been blessed with a very rich and full life even though I haven't had a mate."

The look on my face must have been one of sympathy or grief, because Margaret laughed at me and patted my hand gently.

"Don't look so sad! I'm not."

"I just can't imagine going through life alone like that."

"Oh, but I wasn't alone. God was always with me and good friends, too."

I fidgeted a little. "Uh, right...still...I don't think I could do it."

Margaret used her arms to lift herself off the floor, waving aside my offer of help. "God gives His children the strength to do the things they need to do and to face the things they need to face. You will understand that more clearly after you have met with my son."

My head was dancing with visions and images from years gone by while my arms were full of notes and a tape recorder. We moved toward the door.

"Will you be traveling to Brownsville soon?"

"In a couple of days. I have to get the information you gave me down on paper before I lose the details."

Margaret smiled. "I'd like to see my son's reaction when he hears what I had to say. He will probably have his own interpretation of certain events."

I had to smile in agreement. "I'm sure you're right. Very few parents and children remember events the same way. Well, thank you again for talking with me. I have enjoyed every minute." As an after thought, I turned and asked, "Can I come again sometime…just to visit?"

Margaret seemed pleased by the question. "Call me when you want to talk."

"I will." We exchanged smiles and a quick nod as Margaret closed the door. I walked to my waiting car not understanding why I had asked that last question and puzzled by the fact that I had actually meant it.

Chapter 15

The Jonesborro Street Church proudly proclaimed its birth to be 1880 on a plaque firmly fixed to the wall on the left side of the entrance. Time, weather, and wind had taken their toll on the once cheerful red structure. The color of the bricks had become a mixture of yellow-orange and red-orange mingled with an occasional brown. There were traces here and there of a white residue that suggested an attempt to paint the brick white in years gone by. The paint, too, had fallen pray to the south Texas climate.

Cracks had appeared in the exterior walls and been duly patched with cement creating what looked like large scars on the face of the once proud structure. The double doors were set back in a recess about twelve inches deep. An arch peaked about four feet over the heavy oak paneled doors. Spanish style wrought iron light fixtures were mounted on either side of the entrance.

I lifted my hand to the handle. At last, I was standing on the threshold of the opportunity of my life. On the other side of that door was Jacob Bystander. He was waiting for me and in a few minutes, he would begin unfolding the story of how he had become a leading force in the religious kingdom.

I paused for one last look around me. This was not what I had expected. How could anyone so influential work out of such an old broken down building? The windows, constructed of eight by ten single pane glass, looked like they were the originals. They were set in arched frames of brick, much like the one over the front entry.

"Probably delivered by buckboard." I mused to myself. "What kind of person works in such a place? Only one way to find out." I lifted my hand to the brass knocker and let it fall. The sound was heavy and loud. I listened intently as the barely perceptible shuffle of footsteps approached the door from within.

The heavy door creaked open. I don't know what I expected, but certainly not Jacob Bystander himself. Surely, he had people to answer the door for him.

"Hello. You must be Elizabeth." Jacob extended a hand to me.

I found his handshake as warm and friendly as his smile. *'What charisma,'* I thought. *'No wonder he has such a large following. This man only has to look at you with those eyes of his, speak in that musical voice, and you're hanging on every word.'*

"Come in out of the heat. This old building is much cooler than you might think."

I couldn't help looking up at the vaulted ceiling, with the wrought iron lights suspended from chains, as Jacob closed the door behind me. We walked between two rows of old wooden pews that lined each side of the room. The center aisle lead from the door to a platform at the opposite end. Across the front of the platform was an ornately carved railing that resembled a picket fence without a gate. A piano stood at the back of the platform and on the left. In the middle, was a podium from which, I assumed, sermons were delivered. On each side of this area was a door. I followed Jacob through the one on the right and into his office.

"I trust you didn't have any trouble finding us?" He looked over his shoulder at me.

"No, not at all. The town isn't that large. In fact, it's quite small. I will admit I'm a little surprised that you maintain your headquarters in such an interesting place." I wanted to say 'an antiquated place' but didn't.

Jacob laughed at my remark as he indicated a chair for me. "I guess it does seem a little odd to have my office here." He looked around the room with a wistful kind of expression. "We're a lot alike this place and I...it suits me. You wouldn't know it to look at it but there was a time when this church was in danger of crumbling to the ground. The roof leaked. The windows rattled or were missing panes. The walls were full of cracks. However, the foundation is solid rock, and a building built on rock is built to last."

I tried to see the room as he saw it. It still looked old to me—an antiquated mission with patched walls, refurbished windows, new paint, and throw rugs. I wasn't too sure it was out of danger.

I decided to move on. I indicated my tape recorder. "I hope you don't mind. It helps me keep my facts straight."

"Not at all. Facts are important."

"Will your wife be joining us?"

"She'll be here shortly. She had to run an errand."

Noticing my somewhat bewildered look, Jacob asked, "Is there something on your mind?"

"You answer your own door; your wife runs errands. Where are the others? I mean...you must have people who work for you. There doesn't seem to be anyone else here."

There was that smile again.

"Oh, I see. Let me explain. We used to operate a soup kitchen at this location. Now it serves as our main headquarters. My wife and I work here, and we hold staff meetings in what used to be the sanctuary. Once a week we hold worship services for those who don't feel comfortable going elsewhere. We have a secretary who is here most of the time, but she is on vacation this week."

Now it was my turn to laugh. My nervousness was beginning to subside.

"My wife and I have a sentimental attachment to the place." Jacob looked at the surroundings lovingly. "But I don't want to get ahead of myself." He smiled at me with a twinkle in his eyes that reminded me of his mother. "We couldn't bring ourselves to part with the old girl—you'll understand the reasons later. When we began to outgrow her, we slowly moved different programs and services to other locations. Each of those locations has administrative offices on site. The individual administrators report to me here. This..." He spread his arms as if to embrace the whole mission. "Is what you might call the hub. Everything we do reaches out from here."

I was anxious to get started. "I've read about your different areas of ministry and they're very impressive. However, for today, I thought we might cover some more of the pre-ministry years. I sent you a copy of the information your mother gave me on your childhood. I'd like to pick up where she left off, unless you have anything you want to add to what she has already told me?"

"I don't think I'll try to improve upon what my mother has told you..." Jacob leaned back in his chair, put his hands behind his head, and closed his eyes. "So, where shall I begin?" After a moments recollection, he turned his chair just enough to be able to see out the window. The air of playfulness that he had displayed earlier gave way to one of seriousness. He placed his right arm across his mid-section and propped his left elbow on his right hand. He then began to tap his lips with his finger as he collected his thoughts. When he had at last decided where to begin, Jacob shifted his elbows to the arms of the chair and tapped his fingertips together as he spoke. His eyes never left the window as my tape recorder captured every word.

Chapter 16

The two boys raced through the door nearly tripping over each other and bumping into the wall. They laughed as they went stumbling and falling into their mother's room. Jacob was the first to reach the chest and promptly fell across the top shouting.

"I won! I won!"

Jonas heaved a sigh and plopped on the floor next to the victor. "Only because I let you this time."

"Ha! I won fair and square and you know it!" Jacob gave Jonas a playful shove as he slid off the chest and settled onto the floor next to his brother.

"It doesn't matter. I'll win next time." Jonas turned his attention to the chest. He grew somber as he lifted the lid and viewed its contents. They still fascinated him. It was like a time machine capable of taking him and Jacob on adventures into another world—a world they could never know; yet, a world that shaped their lives and was a part of them.

"I want to wear the vest." Jacob spoke with determination.

"You always wear the moccasins and I wear the vest."

"I know, but I want to switch this time."

"Why?"

Jacob shrugged his shoulders. "No reason in particular. I just want to do something different."

Jonas lifted the neatly folded vest from the corner. "Okay, you won so you get first choice. I'll wear the moccasins."

Jacob jumped to his feet pulling his T-shirt over his head at the same time. He quickly dawned the fringed and beaded vest that had once belonged to William Bystander. It sagged and drooped on his thin body. He straightened the shoulders and sucked in air as he tried to puff out his chest as much as possible. Unfortunately, no matter how much he tried, the vest still hung limp. It had been fashioned for someone much broader.

Jonas laughed as he pulled on the moccasins. "You can't walk around holding your breath like that, and even if you could, it doesn't help. It doesn't fit you any better than it does me."

Jacob released the air that he had been holding as he slumped to the floor beside his brother. He began to pick through the contents of the box until he found a leather pouch. He emptied it on the floor and began to count.

"Why do you do that?"

"...Eighteen, nineteen, twenty, twenty-one. I don't know exactly."

Jacob had placed twenty-one shiny brass shell casings in a neat row on the floor.

Jonas studied the row of casings. "Why do you suppose they use twenty-one? Why not eighteen or twenty or some other number?"

"I don't know. Maybe the first time they gave a twenty-one gun salute, twenty-one bullets were all they had." Jacob picked the casings up one at a time and began to count them again as he put them back into the bag. He pulled the string tight as he returned it to its customary spot.

"Did you ever wonder what are in those letters?" Jacob's gaze lingered on the bundle of faded envelopes tied with an equally faded pink ribbon.

Jonas cast a quick glance in their direction before answering. "Of course, but you know Mom said they were private and she wasn't ready for us to read them."

Jacob let his hand drift in their direction. "I know, but she wouldn't know if we were to sneak a peek?"

Jonas reached out and took hold of Jacob's wrist just as he was about to pick up the forbidden letters. "She'd know. She always knows—and even if she didn't—we would."

"Yeah, you're right."

Jonas loosed his hold on Jacob and reached for a stack of pictures. He studied each one as though he were seeing it for the first time before he passed it to Jacob. He came to one of Margaret and William and held it up.

"I don't think Mom has changed very much; do you?"

Jacob leaned over to get a better look at the picture in Jonas' hand.

"A little."

Jonas held the picture up next to Jacob's face. His eyes moved rapidly from one to the other several times.

"What are you doing?"

"I wanted to see if we look like him."

Jacob took the picture from Jonas' hand. It was his turn to compare brother and picture. "Let me see."

A voice from the doorway spoke.

"I can answer that question."

The boys had been so engrossed in what they were doing that they had not noticed their mother. Margaret had been standing and watching in silence—waiting. She wanted to savor this moment as long as possible. Her boys were growing up and would soon be leaving her. There wouldn't be very many more tender moments of innocence. Indeed, she wondered if that time had not already passed away. At fourteen, how innocent could they be? The hugs and kisses were growing fewer every day. They were more likely to be embarrassed by her affection than they were to return it. Therefore, she drank in this moment—a moment when they were little boys again trying to fill their father's shoes.

"Mom, we didn't hear you come in."

"You both grow to look more and more like your father with each passing year. Sometimes, I look at you and I think he is still with me." Margaret moved to join them on the floor and gently took the picture as Jacob offered it to her. She studied the face of the husband and father who was now only a memory for her and a mystery to them. "His eyes weren't blue like yours. They were such a dark brown that they were almost black. They were the prettiest eyes I have ever seen." She smiled and her face grew soft. "They were magical. They could be cold and piercing like ice when he was angry...But when he was overflowing with passion, they were hotter than fire—hot enough to melt the coldest heart."

In the silence that followed, each of them entertained visions of William. Jacob and Jonas imagined him standing next to them wearing the manly clothing that they tried to fill with their youthful bodies. How tall had he been? Were they approaching his height? Would he have made them vests and moccasins of their own to match his? Would they still be in Seneca roaming the hills and streams together? What would it have been like to have had a father?

Margaret pondered similar questions, but, at the same time, she relived a thousand memories—memories awakened by the smell of buckskin. She, too, wondered what life would have been like if Will had lived. But what profit was there in dreams? They would not bring him back or change the future. There was only now and the problems of today. She pushed aside her daydreams and rejoined the present.

"Well," Margaret hurried to place the pictures in their proper place, all traces of nostalgia quickly fading away. "I need to think about dinner. Are you two getting hungry?" She smiled and rose to her feet, smoothing the lines of her dress before placing her hands on her hips.

"Starving!" It was hard to tell which boy shouted the loudest.

Margaret smiled. "I thought so." She called to them over her shoulder as she started toward the door. "Finish in here as quickly as you can, and put everything away just as you found it." She stopped and turned to them just before passing from view. "By the way, we're going to have a guest for dinner tonight."

Jacob and Jonas looked up with expressions that were a mixture of surprise and astonishment.

"I have invited a gentleman from Church to join us."

Their mouths fell open as a mischievous grin toyed with the corners of Margaret's mouth. "Don't look at me like that. Do you think it so amazing that a man would want to have dinner with me?"

"Who is he?" Jonas asked.

"Do we know him?"

"You met him Sunday. Remember the gentleman I introduced to you right after the service?"

Jacob found his voice first. "No! Mom! Not him!"

They scurried to their feet and approached their mother with arms waving wildly.

"He's crazy!"

"Yeah, he's crazy!"

"Crazy? What are you talking about?" Margaret was puzzled by this sudden outburst. She had not expected such an outpouring of concern.

"Something's weird about him."

"He gives me the creeps." Jacob pretended to shiver.

Margaret smiled in spite of herself. "You're exaggerating."

"No I'm not!" Jacob insisted.

"No, really, Mom, there's something weird about him. I can't put my finger on what; I just know there's something."

The serious and pleading eyes of Jonas melted the smile on Margaret's face. "Well, it's just dinner, and you will both be here to protect me." She cupped a determined chin in each of her hands. "Thank you for being concerned. He's a new Christian and needs friends to encourage him. It's not like I'm planning on marrying him. So cheer up, and be polite." Margaret's eyes grew moist. "My heart is already full..." She took a deep breath and turned away before the looks on their faces could bring her to tears. "And I have a dinner to cook."

Chapter 17

The evening had gone well—considering Jacob and Jonas went out of their way to be underfoot and never out of her sight. They had excelled in the interest they showed to Mr. Moxley. They bombarded him with a never-ending string of questions, some of which bordered on embarrassing. *'Where do you live? Where do you work? Why don't you have a car; was your driver's license taken away? (*He had arrived on a bicycle.) *Have you ever been arrested? What about drugs?'*

More than once, Margaret had to reprimand them for their questions and apologize for their inappropriate curiosity. Thankfully, Mr. Moxley took it all in stride and laughed it all off as *'youthful zeal which was very normal for boys of their age.'*

He left them in good humor declaring what an enjoyable evening he had. He did not, however, express a desire to repeat the evening anytime soon. For this, everyone was grateful, even Margaret. She did not have the energy to face another such ordeal in the near future.

When the door finally closed on their dinner guest, Margaret turned her attention to her boys. They didn't need to see the anger in her eyes to know they were in trouble. The set of her jaw, the firm lines around her mouth, and the stiffness of her shoulders were enough to cause them to try for a hasty retreat from the scene of the crime.

"Good night, Mom." Jacob was already headed down the hall.

"Good night, Mom." Jonas echoed his brother and was two steps behind him and closing.

"Hold it!" Came the command in that unmistakable tone that they dared not ignore.

They stopped in their tracks and looked at each other with the same thought passing between them-*'We're going to get it now.'*

"You two come over here and sit down. I want to talk to you." She was fuming.

'Here it comes.' They thought. *'The lecture. A beating would be more bearable. It would be quicker and easier to forget.'* They tried to look properly repentant, but, in reality, they would do it all again if given the chance. They believed they were right to protect their mother from guys like that Mr. Moxley. After all, they were the men of the house. They knew more about men than she did. It was their duty to watch out for her. They had used the best means available to them to get rid of the guy.

"Don't ever be that rude to a guest in my house again. He was supposed to feel welcome; instead, you acted as though he was the enemy and this was an inquisition. How could you do that?" She waited not really expecting an answer. They gave none. "How would you like to go into a stranger's house and have two children bombard you with the same type of questions you were dishing out here tonight?" Again, she waited.

Jacob and Jonas hung their heads and stared at the floor. They knew she wouldn't like their answer—*'If I didn't have anything to hide, I wouldn't mind.'* They didn't want to lie, so they said nothing.

"What could you have been thinking?"

This question genuinely seemed to require an answer. Jonas spoke what was on the heart of both.

"We were afraid."

"Afraid of what?" Margaret was puzzled.

"We were afraid you might become interested in him."

"Actually, we were afraid you might become interested in someone—anyone." Jonas was choosing his words carefully. "We had never thought about the possibility of you getting married before. All of a sudden," he waived his hand at the front door, "this guy was coming for dinner."

"I guess we panicked." Jacob shrugged his shoulders.

Margaret suddenly felt very tired, very old, and very lonely. She sank into the couch and leaned her head back until it rested on the soft cushions. She closed her eyes and felt the moisture build behind her lids. After a moment, she spoke in a hushed tone void of emotion.

"Go to bed."

They went to their room as quietly and quickly as they could, leaving their mother alone with her thoughts. Presently, she brushed away a tear that had managed to escape from under her eyelid. Never had Seneca seemed so far away as it did at that moment. Never had she missed the wise and steadfast Sadie as much she did now. She needed a shoulder to cry on, and she had none.

From their room, Jacob and Jonas listened. The house was as quiet as a tomb. Occasionally, they could hear a sniff, which meant their mother was crying. Why did she have to do that? Didn't she know that they couldn't stand to see or hear her cry? It was torture. It made them feel helpless.

Shortly, they heard the door to her room open then close. After that, they heard the sound of something dragged across the floor. In their mind's-eye, the boys could see her lift the lid of the box. She would now take out the letters, untie the ribbon, and read them for the hundredth time.

"Jacob?"

"I know. I know."

"She's reading those letters again."

They waited in the darkness for what they knew would come next. The same pattern as many times before. She would read the letters one by one, then cry herself to sleep. She never let them see her cry, but they knew she did. The puffy eyes and red nose the next day told on her.

"Jonas, do you think Mom is lonely?"

Jonas lay on his back with his hands behind his head. He stared at the ceiling thinking.

"I don't know...maybe...probably."

Jacob rested on his side; his elbow and hand supported his head. He looked across his brother and fixed his eyes on the closed door as though, by doing so, he could see into the next room.

"Were we wrong for what we did?"

Jonas considered the question. "We were right to care; we were wrong to be rude." He shifted onto his side in order to face his brother. "But I'll tell you one thing, I'd do the same thing again if I thought she was interested in someone like that Moxley. She's not dumb, but she doesn't know men the way we do."

Jacob totally agreed. "Right. There's something not right about him."

They shared a mischievous grin in the dark.

"I bet he doesn't come to dinner again."

"I bet he doesn't either. Put it there brother."

They slapped the palms of their hands together in a 'high-five' before settling in for the night. Considering themselves completely vindicated of any wrongdoing where Mr. Moxley was concerned, the two partners in crime soon drifted off to sleep undisturbed by any pangs of guilt. After all, they could boast of just and right motives and a clear conscience.

Across the hall, Margaret sat on the floor at the foot of her bed. Before her sat Will's box. She ran her hand over the lid tenderly tracing the letters carved on its face. Eventually, she opened the lid and began to survey its contents. Her hands went to the letters—just as they always did.

Hours passed before Margaret returned the letters to their resting-place. She closed the lid on the past and retraced the letters of Will's name once again with her fingertips. Her lower lip began to quiver. She spread both her arms across the top of the chest, lifted her eyes to heaven, and cried out to God. "How much...How much must I endure? I can't do this alone. Help me to do the right thing. There's so much at stake. How can I trust my own wisdom? There are so many things to draw them away and steal their lives. I don't want to be alone; yet...I am. I didn't plan my life this way. I never dreamed it would be like this. I want to have a husband and a father for the boys, but it hasn't happened. I guess you want it this way, but I don't understand why." The tears were spilling over and running down Margaret's cheeks as she laid her head on the chest. Then a small voice inside her head said, *'My ways are not your ways, and My thoughts are not your thoughts. You need only trust and obey.'*

'Trust and obey.' The words echoed over and over in Margaret's brain. *'Trust and obey.'* She wiped the tears from her face with her hands and sniffed. *'Trust and obey.'* If God had not sent someone to her who could stir her heart

the way Will had, then He must intend for her to rely solely on Him.

Margaret's mind raced back to those early years in Seneca with Johnny and Sadie. They had been there to help her. The time with them had allowed her to gain strength and confidence, although, she didn't feel very confident right now. Still, she knew she was stronger than she had been. Time had marched on, and the trials had gotten tougher.

Margaret grew calmer as she remembered something that Sadie had once told her. *'A person's walk with God was either like a pond or like a river. In a pond, the water doesn't go anywhere. It doesn't move. It grows stale and stagnant. Moss grows in the water, and it's not very inviting for swimming. But a river is always moving and flowing somewhere. Wherever the lay of the land leads, whether it is down the mountain, through valleys, or across the plains, the river is making its way to the open sea or the ocean. Rivers have direction. Their water is fresh and clear because flowing over rocks cleanses it. A river is far more appealing to a swimmer than a pond. Its path is never smooth; the rocks are always there, but...it's better to be a river than a pond.'*

Margaret was at peace again. She shoved the self-pity aside and quietly lay down to sleep. She would meet tomorrow's rocks with God at her side just as she had been doing everyday since Will had died. Someday she would finish the journey; she would reach the ocean, and it would have been worth it all.

Chapter 18

"What do you think you're doing?" Jonas watched as Jacob picked up the stack of letters tied with the faded pink ribbon.

"What does it look like."

"You can't read those. They're private. Mom doesn't want us to read them. You know that."

Jacob stopped and looked at Jonas with a scowl on his face.

"Don't pretend that you don't want to know what's in them, because I know you do. These letters are the only things that can tell us about our parents and their life together. I want to know my father. I want to know what he thought when he was young." Jacob hesitated before he went on. When he spoke again, his voice was softer and lower. "I want to know what made him so special that Mom has never wanted to get married again. Don't you wonder the same thing? I mean…haven't you thought about it?"

"Of course I've thought about it. I know she's not a spring chicken, but she was only twenty-one when Dad died. That's only six years older than us." Jonas thought about all the cute girls at school, and the palms of his hands began to sweat. The idea of *NEVER* having a girlfriend or getting married was unthinkable.

"We'll just read a few then put them back just the way they were. She'll never know we read them."

Jonas shook his head in a feeble protest. "I don't feel right about this, Jacob. They weren't meant for others to read."

"It was a long time ago." Jacob's hand was already opening the first envelope. He knew Jonas was as curious as he was. "Look, I'll tell you what, if we start reading and they are too personal, we'll stop, okay?"

"Okay." Was all Jonas said, his eyes focused on the faded letter in Jacob's hands.

Their hearts raced and nervous sweat began to break out on their foreheads as the words came to life.

My Dearest Will,

> *I miss you more than ever today. I miss your smile and your laughing eyes. I miss the way you used to hold me, and I miss your kisses. But I think I miss the sound of your voice most of all.*
>
> *The sound of you singing in the shower or in the kitchen used to fill my heart with such warmth that words alone cannot hope to express it. When you held me in your arms and sang softly to me, my heart drank in every word and every note until I was sure that it would burst.*
>
> *I try to be strong and patient, but patience was never my best virtue, as you well know. I pray daily that the torture of this separation will end soon, and I will be in your arms again.*
>
> *Until I can join you there, hold your pillow in your arms, and I'll hold mine close to me. Sing to me. I'll listen with my heart and hear your voice. When you do, the miles between us*

will fade away, and we'll be together in spirit and soul.

All my love forever and always, Maggie.

Neither boy said a word. Jacob folded the letter and returned it to its envelope. He gave one quick glance at Jonas before opening the one addressed to their mother. It began…

My Darling Maggie,

The days are long and lonely here without you. I stay busy, but work can't keep you from my thoughts. I put your picture near my bunk. Your lovely face greets me each morning and tucks me in each night. I sometimes find myself humming one of your favorite tunes in the darkness and imagine I can smell the scent of your hair.

My heart aches for you so much that I sometimes think I can't bear it another minute. But God gives me strength to face each day and the peace of mind to know that each day that passes brings me one day closer to being with you again.

I try to convince myself that my present misery will someday be a long faded memory that was only a tiny speck of time in our long life together. I have not succeeded yet, but I'll keep trying. In the meantime, know that I love

*you dearly and will never be content until I
have you by my side.*

Forever and always, Will

"That's enough. I don't want to hear anymore."

"Yeah, me either." Jacob carefully replaced the letter and retied the ribbon. He then deposited the love letters in their former resting-place.

"I don't think I'll ever be able to look Mom in the face again without feeling embarrassed." Jonas' young face wore a very sober look.

"I know what you mean. I had no idea that they talked like that. I thought that stuff was just in the movies. Can you imagine our mother..."

"No, and I don't want to try." Jonas held up his hand to his brother and shook his head. "I told you they were too personal and we should leave them alone. Now we're going to look guilty and Mom's going to know we did something."

"How's she going to know?"

Jonas pulled out the vest and began to unbutton his shirt. "I don't know, but she always seems to know when we've done something we shouldn't. I wish I hadn't let you talk me into reading them."

"You were just as curious as I was and you know it. So stop trying to act like it was all my idea."

"You're right. Let's just try to forget it. I'm wearing the vest today. Let's go meet the guys. Maybe that will help take our minds off those letters."

Jacob fished around in the chest and pulled out a beaded leather headband. "I think I'll wear this. I'd wear the moccasins but I don't want to wear them out." He tied it around his forehead and turned to Jonas for approval. "How does this look?"

"Stupid. Tie it around your forearm instead. An arm band is cooler."

Jacob pulled the ties loose and wrapped the leather band around his left forearm. "I can't tie with one hand. You'll have to do it."

"It's a little big for your arm. I'll wrap the strings around twice so they won't hang down so far…there…now we're ready to roll."

The two renegades smiled at each other while they made a conscious effort not to look at the bundle of letters tied with ribbon. They hastily shut the lid and raced out the door to find their friends as they tried to push thoughts of singing and pillows and scented hair to the back of their minds.

Chapter 19

"Did you get it?" Tom asked eagerly.

Nick held up a brown paper sack. "Piece of cake." A grin spread across his face. "I stole it from my old man."

It was the custom of the group to draw straws whenever someone was going on an "assignment." The assignment this day had been to get a six-pack of beer. It had been Nick's responsibility to decide how to accomplish the task.

"All right!" The gang of boys, who had been sitting quietly in a shed behind Tom's house, suddenly came to life.

"Who's got the key?"

"Here." Willie opened his bottle, took a gulp, and tossed Rob the opener in one smooth movement that only comes from practice.

The key, as they called it, made the rounds until it finally came to the Bystander brothers. Unlike the other guys, they had not been raised around alcohol and had never tasted beer. Jonas looked at Jacob. He knew just by the expression on his brother's face that they were thinking the same thing. *'What if Mom finds out?'* They knew she would be furious with them. *'Was it worth the risk?'*

"Are you gonna drink it or just look at it?" Willie snickered from his perch on a wooden crate. All eyes watched the two brothers.

Jacob opened his bottle; spray shot into the air and foam ran over the side. He handed the key to Jonas. "I like to drink mine slow." The decision was made—better to risk Mother's wrath than face the scorn and ridicule of the gang.

Jonas watched as Jacob lifted the container to his lips and took his first sip. A slight twitch in the corner of his eye was the only reaction Jacob gave to the odd bitter taste. He lowered it and held it at arms length as if to study the brand label. With a very serious face he said, "Not bad...It's not the brand I'm used to, but it's not bad."

Jonas rolled his eyes and pursed his lips while the rest of the group burst into a roar of laughter. Willie slapped his knee with his empty hand as he hung his head down and shook it from side to side. "I'll tell you what, Jake, you are too funny for words! Admit it! You never drank a beer before have ya?"

Jacob didn't answer.

Willie got to his feet and sauntered over to the brothers. He stood between them with his arms resting across their shoulders. "You know what I think we should do? I think we should have a party and initiate these two. And I think they should bring the refreshments."

There was a round of cheers from the other boys as Willie continued. "And since you're so new at this, I'm gonna tell you how it's done." Willie wove his way in and out among the gang members as he spoke. "Old man Miller keeps beer in a cooler on his back porch. One of you go to the front and keep Miller busy while the other one slips in the back and lifts two six packs outa the cooler." Willie had worked his way back to the brothers and stood facing them. "Simple. Don't you think Chief?" Willie stretched out his hand and flipped the beads on Jonas' vest.

Jacob saw Jonas' jaw stiffen and knew without looking that his fists were clinched. He felt his own temperature rise in anger. He firmly pushed Willie's hand away. "The name is Jonas and we can do our own thinking."

A smirky grin appeared on Willie's face as he threw his hands in the air in a mock surrender. Stepping back he said, "Whatever you say, I was only trying to give you a suggestion."

"Come on, Jonas." Jacob nudged his brother as he pushed past Willie. Most of the time Jonas was easy-going, but the cold piercing glare that he had fixed on Willie betrayed his inner struggle for control. "We'll be back later with the stuff." The four boys watched in silence as the two brothers disappeared out the door and around the corner.

Once they were away from the prying eyes of the gang, Jonas pulled Jacob up short. "What was that all about?"

"What was what all about?"

"You know what I mean. Since when do you back away from a fight?" Although Jonas was not as angry as he had been, his words were still laced with emotion. "He was making fun of us! Calling you 'Jake' and me 'Chief.' Don't tell me that it didn't bother you, because I know it did!" Jonas poked Jacob in the shoulder with his finger as he spoke.

Jacob turned on his heel and kicked at the ground. "Of course it bothered me! But they don't mean anything by it. Everyone talks like that around here. You know that. We just have to be one of the guys—like them—then they'll respect us."

"Yeah, I know." Jonas shook his fist at Jacob. "But if he ever touches my vest again…he's gonna get it!"

Jacob couldn't help but laugh. "Now there's a switch! You ready to fight and me the calm one!"

Jonas couldn't help laughing, too. "Yeah, that is funny, huh. But I mean it. Anymore cracks from any of them…and…" He smacked his fist into his open palm.

"Only if you beat me to it!"

Jacob threw his arm around Jonas as they started down the street again. "Now about this beer—do you have a better plan than the one Willie suggested?"

"Sure do—go home and forget it."

"We can't do that. We'd look like sissies."

"Do you want to be a puppet? Since when do we follow orders from the likes of Willie? Do you think cowering to him will earn respect?"

"You have a point, but if we don't do something we'll look like cowards. So, what do we do?"

"How about a compromise?"

"Like what?"

Jonas was stroking his chin thinking. "What if we get the beer without stealing it, and then we give it to them when we decide and not when they demand it?"

Jacob thought about the idea. "Keep it sort of legal and on our terms, right?"

"That's the idea. And...we don't have to drink any if we don't want to either."

Jacob made an ugly face. "I don't see what they like about it...I guess it has to grow on you."

The two brothers walked on down the street forming their plans. It was simple really. All they had to do was find a ride across the state line—Oklahoma being a dry state—get someone to buy beer for them, and then get a ride back, but who?

Jonas smiled. "Why not Mr. Miller? He's always drinking. He must make a lot of trips to Kansas."

Jacob shrugged. "Sounds good to me. Let's try it. How much money do we need?" Both boys started digging in their pockets. Between them, they had $3.86.

"Do you think it's enough?" Jacob wondered.

"Let's go talk to Mr. Miller; he'll know."

Mr. Miller was a World War I veteran who lived alone in a shabby little house about a mile away. He drank most of the time and it was always best to catch him early in the day before the alcohol had completely clouded his mind. By evening he was usually too drunk to stay awake or make much sense. His health wasn't very good, but he still managed to putter around doing little jobs here and there as a handyman. He was still quite good with his hands.

The walk was a short one for the brothers from Seneca, and they soon found themselves in front of Mr. Miller's door. "Here goes." Jonas knocked…Nothing…He knocked again…Still nothing. The two boys looked at each other before Jonas knocked a third time. They were about to give up when Mr. Miller came around the corner of the house.

"I thought I heard someone round here?" Mr. Miller staggered and limped up the steps. The limp was from a war injury, but the stagger was a combination of age and alcohol. He patted Jacob on the back. "Good to see you boys. What brings you out my way today?"

"We were just hangin' around with nothing to do and we thought we'd stop by and say hi." Jonas stuffed his hands in his pockets to hide his uneasiness.

Jacob followed Jonas' lead. "Yeah, what you been doin' with yourself Mr. Miller? Workin' hard?"

Mr. Miller plopped down in a wicker chair that had seen a great deal of use. He pulled a handkerchief from his pocket and began wiping his face and neck. "I'll tell you boys, it has been mighty hot lately and I'm not as young as I used to be. This ol' heat fairly wears me down. Say, Jacob, why don't you hop out to the back porch and grab a beer for me from that old cooler." Mr. Miller was one of the few people who could tell the difference in the two boys.

"Sure thing, Mr. Miller." Jacob hurried through the door and was back again in only a minute or two. He handed the cold drink to the old man. "Here you go, sir, nice and cold."

The veteran of many beers leaned forward and artfully opened the bottle on the porch railing. He had positioned it just right before giving it a swift smack with his hand. The top had popped right off. The boys watched in admiration.

"Whoa! I've never seen anybody do that before."

Mr. Miller lifted his free hand in the air and gave a little wave. "It's all in the wrist...and practice...lots of practice." He grinned sheepishly.

"Can I try?" Jonas saw a chance to steer the conversation toward Kansas.

"Sure...just let me finish this one and you can open the next one." With that, he put the bottle to his lips and in a few gulps had downed the entire contents. He sighed deeply and set the bottle on the porch. "Better save that. They charge a deposit for the bottles you know."

"You mean like they do for pop bottles?" Jacob was mentally counting the cost of twelve bottle deposits at two cents each.

"Sure do. It's a nuisance, but, hey, what's a little nuisance compared to the product, eh?" He leaned forward and patted the porch rail as if it were a good dog. "All I need are a few cold ones and a little edge of anything." He gave the rocker a little push. "Fetch me another and you can give it a try."

Jonas ran for the back porch and quickly returned with two bottles. He handed one to Jacob. "Okay, I hold it like this…right?" Jonas tried to duplicate the way he had seen Mr. Miller hold the bottle.

The expert eyed the angle. "Hold it down a little more. You hold it to flat and the glass'll break. You want the edge of the cap right on the edge of the wood. That's better. Now just give it a little whack."

"How hard?" Jonas was nervous. What if he broke it?

"About as hard as you'd slap the rump of a horse to get him movin'."

Jonas held his breath and smacked the glass. Off came the top followed by foam, which spilled over the top. "I did it! I did it!" Jonas was all smiles as he handed the beer to its rightful owner.

"You did good." Mr. Miller leaned back and downed a couple of swallows.

"Can I try next?"

"Give me a chance to finish this one first." He chuckled to himself. "Unless, of course, you planned on drinking it yourself?"

Jacob and Jonas laughed nervously. "Well, do you think you have enough to go around? We wouldn't want you to run out."

Mr. Miller seemed to become a little more sober at the comment. He stopped rocking and looked sideways at them with one eye squinted in thought. He didn't know if they were serious or kidding. "How old are you boys?"

"Fifteen."

"Going on sixteen." Jacob considered any time past one birthday as 'going on' the next one. It didn't matter that it would be eleven more months.

"Fifteen, huh. Well, I was pretty curious at that age—
best I can remember. I might let you have one bottle to
share. How many were left when you brought these out?"

"Just two."

"Two! Great day in the mornin'! I don't even have
enough to last the day! Well, only one thing to do. I'll jest
have to get me some more."

"How do you get beer when Oklahoma is dry?" Jacob
asked innocently.

"I jest drive up into Kansas..." he waved his hand north
"and bring it back. Takes a few hours, but it's worth it.
Only other option for a feller what wants a drink is buying
the rot gut moonshine that the bootleggers peddle around
here. Stuff'll make you go blind fur sure. Nope, the only
thing to do is get the real stuff from Kansas." He pushed
himself up out of his chair. "Say, Jonas, how 'bout gettin'
me those last two beers for the trip."

"Uh, Mr. Miller, can we ride along with you?" Jacob
ventured while Jonas went after the beer.

"Sure, boy. I'd like the company. Pile in!"

Jonas returned and all three climbed into a beat up old
forty something Chevy truck. It was crowded, and Jonas
was stuck in the middle with the stick shift between his
knees.

"Coming back...you get the middle." Jonas said under
his breath as the knob on the stick vibrated against his knee.

Off they went—the three of them. It was a fairly
uneventful trip, and much sooner than they expected, they
were there—a little square concrete block building thrown
together specifically for the purpose of selling beer to
people from Oklahoma. It was only a few yards across the
state line.

Mr. Miller was in a jolly mood. Perhaps now was a good time to approach him about buying beer for them. Jonas began.

"You know, I've been giving it some thought. I don't think it's fair for us to drink your beer and not put in any money for it. How about we pitch in some money?"

"Well now that's a mighty fine idea."

"How much does beer cost?"

"Around $1.25 plus the deposit for a six pack. Two bits will cover one bottle easy."

"We've been thinking. We have about six weeks before school starts. What if we buy two six packs—one each—and then we'll have enough for one bottle a week."

The old man thought it over. "Sure, why not." Perhaps if he had been a little more sober or a little less drunk, he would have acted differently. As it was, he took the money given to him, made his purchase and theirs, and was soon behind the wheel of the truck headed home.

The ride back was different. The days intake of alcohol was beginning to take its toll. Mr. Miller drove a little too fast and often strayed into the middle of the road. Once or twice he even drifted off onto the shoulder—what there was of it. More than once Jacob reached up and started to grab the wheel. Each time, Mr. Miller corrected himself just in time.

Then it happened. They were on a long stretch of road bordered on each side by open fields. Jacob hesitated too long and Mr. Miller reacted too slowly. The pickup went sailing off the side of the road and into the middle of a freshly plowed field.

"Whoa! I must have hit some loose gravel! Good thing I wasn't drivin' fast—might've got hurt!" He patted the dash. "Good ol' truck. Tough as nails…just like me." He turned a blurry eye and crooked grin to the two stunned boys. "Say, you two weren't scared were ya?"

Neither spoke for a minute. They were still trying to recover. Finally, Jacob found his voice. "Nah, we drive through fields all the time."

Mr. Miller slapped Jacob on the back and gave him a good-natured shake. "Yur right. I guess I shouldn't be driving. How 'bout you drivin' the rest of the way?"

"Me? I don't know how."

"Then now's a good time to learn."

"Are you serous?" Jonas was wide-eyed with surprise.

"Sure! Who's first?" Mr. Miller opened the door and practically fell out as he offered the seat behind the wheel to the brothers. Jacob didn't waste any time sliding his leg from around the stick shift and moving into the drivers seat. The old man laughed. "I guess it's settled." He took the next few minutes to explain the clutch and the gears to Jacob. He let the boy practice shifting while the engine was off. When he felt satisfied that Jacob was ready, he stepped back and closed the door. He hopped up on the running board as he explained, "I'll just ride out here so's I can give ya instructions and…" He grinned and winked at Jonas…"and bail out if the ride gets too rough." He laughed again. "Ok, start 'er up."

Jacob turned the key and the truck sputtered its way to life. He pushed on the pedal and let out the clutch. The motor promptly died.

"You forgot to put 'er in gear. Push in the clutch and try again. Shift into first before you let out the clutch."

The second try was better. The truck jumped and jerked a few feet before it died. The motion had caught Mr. Miller off guard and thrown him onto the ground. He picked himself up, dusted himself off, and remounted the running board.

"That time was better, but a little rough. Guess I better hold on tighter." He made an exaggerated show of clinging to the door before patting Jacob on the shoulder. "It's ok son, it'll be like second nature before the end of the day. Now, this time ease up on the clutch a little slower and wait until the truck is movin' smooth before you let 'er go completely." With a wave of his hand, Mr. Miller gave Jacob the 'go ahead.'

The third time was the charm. Jacob did what he was told and in only a couple of minutes he had shifted his way through first and second, and was settled into third gear. The pickup sailed around in a wide circle throwing a cloud of dirt in its wake. Inside the truck, the two boys were whooping and yelling. On the outside, the old man was holding on for dear life and shouting. "Watch out for those bumps! Don't want to break the cargo or my neck!"

When Jacob had made a couple of rounds, Jonas began to insist on his turn. Jacob pulled to a stop and traded places with his brother. Mr. Miller dropped to the ground and staggered a bit. "Whah! My legs are a little shaky from that ride. Tell ya what, Jonas, I'm gonna take me a beer and go sit at a safe distance and watch." He pulled a bottle from the sack and popped off the top. A couple of gulps latter, he continued. "Jacob here can help ya if ya need it, and ya already heard the same instructions I gave him, so..." He waved his hand behind him as he walked away. "Have at it. I'm gonna rest."

With Jonas behind the wheel this time, the two boys took off again. Having watched Jacob's first efforts, Jonas was able to avoid making the same mistakes. In less time than his brother, he was sailing around the field following the path his brother had traveled before him.

"Wow! This is great! Who would have thought this morning that by the end of the day we would be driving!" Jacob was bubbling with excitement.

"Yeah. It has been a day all right, but we better think about getting home."

"Guess you're right."

Jonas steered over to the spot where Mr. Miller was sitting and watching. The veteran of many drinking campaigns got to his feet as they approached. He staggered a little as he dropped the empty bottle into the back of the truck. "Move over Jacob and let an old man in." He slid in beside Jacob and closed the heavy door before pulling out another bottle. "Do you know the way home?"

Jonas answered. "Yes sir."

Mr. Miller put the drink to his lips as he motioned with a wave of his hand to get moving. Jonas shifted into first and eased his way back onto the road. In no time at all, the three were cruising peacefully toward home, Jonas behind the wheel, Jacob in the middle with the stick shift nestled between his knees, and Mr. Miller half dozing with a bottle cradled in his lap.

"Now I know you don't think you're going to drive all the way back." Jacob scowled at Jonas.

Jonas just smiled as he kept his eyes on the road ahead and pointed the truck, its passengers, and its cargo south.

Chapter 20

The Bystander brothers hurried the ten blocks back to their house. Their attempts at looking casual failed as each one held a sack suspiciously tucked under his arm. They raced along the street their hearts pounding from the day's events.

Finally, they were home.

"Okay, now what do we do?" Jacob wanted to know.

Jonas looked at the clock on the kitchen wall. "Mom is going to be home soon. We better hide this stuff for now and catch up with the guys later."

"Well, we can't hide it in here. Mom will find it for sure."

Jonas hurried to their bedroom. He stood in the doorway and surveyed the room. "You got any ideas?"

"I don't have time to be creative if that's what you mean. Let's just put it in the closet until after dinner. We can sneak it out through the window after Mom's asleep."

Jonas hurried to the closet. He opened the door and quickly scanned the interior for a secure spot. A stack of blankets on a shelf at the top of the closet offered the best cover. He shoved them to one side and pushed the two sacks containing the beer all the way to the back before pulling the blankets back into place. He stepped back a bit and tried to see if the sacks showed.

"What do you think? Think she'll notice anything if she looks in here?"

Before Jacob had a chance to answer, a loud knock on the front door caused both boys to jump. Jonas slammed the closet door shut as Jacob rushed to see who was knocking.

It was Willie and the rest of the guys.

The momentary relief that both brothers felt at the sight of their friends was quickly replaced with a new worry. Jacob opened the door and the brothers stepped out onto the porch.

"What are you doing here? I thought we were supposed to meet you back at Tom's?" Jacob's voice betrayed his irritation. This was very bad timing on Willie's part. Their mother was due home any minute and she was not fond of the guys in the gang. Their presence would only make her suspicious and less likely to let them out of the house.

"What kind of hello is that for friends?" Willie leaned back against the porch post and folded his arms. "We've been waiting at Tom's for a very long time."

"You'll ruin everything if Mom drives up and sees you here." Jonas looked down the street nervously.

Nick moved forward a little and asked in a demanding voice, "Did you get it?"

"Yes, we did, but we'll have to bring it later. You need to go before…"

Jacob glanced over the heads of the gang and saw the familiar sedan turn the corner. He nudged Jonas with his elbow. "Jonas."

"Oh, no." All attention turned in the direction of the car sliding into the driveway. "We'll meet you at Tom's as soon as we can get out of the house. Now get going."

Willie reached out and slapped Jonas on the shoulder before leaving the porch to join his gang. "Later my man." The group of boys sauntered across the yard and turned down the sidewalk as Margaret opened her car door.

Margaret had seen Jacob and Jonas standing on the porch with several boys as she approached. Something in the scene seemed wrong to her, but she didn't know what. Perhaps it was the sober faces of the group. Perhaps it was the way they hurried to leave when they saw her coming, or perhaps it was just her distrust of these new friends that made her suspect they were up to something. Whether it made sense or was reasonable wasn't important. Margaret just didn't like those boys and was glad to see them leave without her sons.

The brothers exchanged a glance before going to greet their mother.

"Hi, Mom." The words were filled with a forced air of lightheartedness that Margaret new was false.

"Is something wrong?" Margaret looked from one to the other. They pumped themselves up and pasted on fake smiles as they tried to laugh off the question and avoid her piercing eyes.

"Wrong? What do you mean? There's nothing wrong, is there Jacob?" They squirmed under her perceptive gaze.

"No, nothing, nothing at all." Jonas tried to imitate his brother's carefree tone as he shrugged his shoulders and stuffed his hands in his pockets.

"Uh, huh." Was all Margaret had to say as she walked toward the house. She knew they were lying. She looked down the street at the boys who had only a few moments before stood on her porch steps. They were hurrying away with their somber faces lost in conversation. She watched as one of them glanced back over his shoulder. He quickly turned back again when he saw her watching. She turned to her boys and nodded her head in the direction of the disappearing group.

"Why did your friends leave in such a hurry when I arrived?"

Still trying to play innocent, each displayed his best wide-eyed look as they searched their brains for a response. They knew their mother could practically read their minds. She always seemed to know before they did what was going to happen.

"They said they had somewhere else to go." Jacob watched Jonas roll his eyes and shake his head.

"Uh huh."

There it was again. How they hated that 'uh huh'! They knew what it meant. It meant she knew they were hiding something. It meant she didn't believe them. It meant they would have a tough time getting out of the house.

Margaret looked from one to the other before giving one last passing glance at the group of boys now fading from sight. She turned on her heel and went into the house calling over her shoulder as she went. "I hope you planned on helping with dinner tonight. Better get washed up and meet me in the kitchen."

Kitchen duty, which could mean only one thing— questions followed by a lecture.

"Great." Jacob murmured under his breath.

"We better get our story straight. You know she's going to ask us what we did today."

"We could tell her the truth…or at least part of it."

"Which part?" Jonas thought over the events of the day.

"The part about learning to drive. We could say we were learning to drive so we could get jobs. She'll like that."

"Sounds good but what kind of jobs?"

"I don't know—maybe on a farm. There's lots of farms around here that need summer help."

Jonas opened the screen door. "Okay. We'll go with that. We better get inside before Mom comes looking for us."

Jacob groaned. "Kitchen duty, yuk."

They hurried to the bathroom to wash their hands.

"Don't make such a fuss. It's not so bad. You like to cook and the cleanup goes fast when you have help."

Jacob puckered his mouth a little bit. "I suppose. But I still don't like it."

Jonas stopped in the middle of drying his hands, placed one hand on his hip, and started shaking his finger at Jacob. He used a high-pitched voice, imitating their mother, "Some things in life we do because they are right and not because they are fun or easy."

Jacob started to laugh. He jerked the towel off the rack and gave it a couple of twists before he flipped it at Jonas. He was too slow however, and Jonas jumped out of range.

"Ha! Missed me!"

Jacob was getting ready to try again when he suddenly stopped and began putting the towel back on the rack. His playful attitude disappeared. Jonas knew even before he looked that their mother was standing behind him.

"I'm so glad you remember what I say."

That was all she said—it was enough. She hesitated only a second or two, as she held them hostage in that stern glare of hers, before turning back to the kitchen.

After she was gone, Jonas punched Jacob in the arm. "Why didn't you tell me she was there?"

Jacob punched him back. "Because I didn't see her until it was too late." He began to chuckle as he remembered

Jonas' impersonation of their mother. "Man you have lousy timing. You're always getting caught."

Jonas followed Jacob out of the bathroom. "Can I help it if I don't have your knack for being sneaky."

"Knack, nothin'! It's skill." Jacob puffed out his chest and raised his chin in the air.

"Skill!" Jonas scoffed. "Too bad you don't have more brains to equal your fat head!" Jonas reached out and mussed Jacob's hair as he rushed past him into the kitchen.

Chapter 21

The evening had gone pretty much as expected. Margaret asked a multitude of questions. The boys gave their version of what they had been doing all day—leaving out selected details—and, as expected, they did not leave the house again that day.

Margaret had been surprised and a little concerned at the news her boys had learned to drive. She would have been even more concerned if she had known all the facts, but the tale that they told was much tamer than the truth. She was especially pleased to hear that they were looking for jobs. Work would help keep them away from 'those' boys.

The evening had passed without too many questions and the hour had finally grown late enough for everyone to go to bed. The night had gone to sleep. Outside the only thing stirring was an occasional car and a stray cat or two. Inside the Bystander house, all was quiet except for the steady hum of the fan in their mother's room. Margaret had turned out her light some time ago and the brothers lay patiently waiting for the right moment to sneak out of the house.

Jacob rose up on one elbow and whispered as quietly as he could. "Jonas?"

"Yes," came the barely audible reply.

"Do you think she's asleep yet?"

Jonas turned his head and tried to see the clock on the table between their beds. It was too dark. He held it up and let the moonlight shine on its face. "I haven't heard any movement from her room for about twenty minutes. If we're very quiet I think we can make it."

"Do you think they're still waiting?"

"I doubt it, but I want to get that stuff out of the house before Mom finds it."

"How could she find it?"

"I don't know, but if we leave it here she will." Jonas was sitting on the side of his bed with his face only inches away from Jacob's face. "We can take it to Tom's and leave it in the shed." Jonas began to move cautiously across the floor avoiding spots that he new would creak. He eased open the closet door. The brothers caught their breath as a tiny squeak was amplified in the stillness.

"Why does everything in this house have to make so much noise?" Jacob took the first sack as Jonas passed it to him. He tried not to rustle the paper but it was impossible. "We should have taken them out of the sacks."

"It's too late now." Jonas passed Jacob the second one. "Hold them as still as you can."

"What do you think I'm doing!"

"It sounds like you're running through leaves or something." Jonas threw the blankets back into place and closed the door. He fairly ran across the room on his way to the window. Squeaky floorboards were forgotten as his heart began to pound at the thought of being caught. "Let's get going. I want to get this over with." Jonas gave the screen on the window a gentle push, and it popped right off. In a few more seconds, he was outside, and Jacob was handing him the goods.

"I can't believe Mom didn't hear us with all the noise we made." Jacob dropped to the ground next to his brother.

"I can't either." Jonas handed one sack to Jacob. "I guess she sleeps sounder than we thought. Let's go."

They half grinned at each other in the moonlight. Fear of discovery had made them tense. Now that they had successfully made their escape, the fear was gone. In its place was a sense of achievement, even pride.

They laughed at themselves and joked about this new adventure. How easy it had been. They imagined all kinds of possibilities for the future. They were having a grand time. So grand in fact that they failed to notice a police car tucked quietly in an alley.

The officer in the car watched them stroll past with their sacks cradled in their arms. Something in the shape of those sacks and the way they were being carried peaked his interest. He looked at his watch—11: 00 p.m.—a bit late for two young boys to be out and about. *'I think I'll just see what they're doing.'* He let them get around the corner before starting his car. Then he crept out slowly onto the street.

The brothers were so intent on their destination that they didn't notice the car until it was practically next to them. "Hello, boys. What are you doing out so late?"

"We're just on our way home, officer." Jacob tried to sound innocent.

"Where have you been?" The officer stopped the car and got out.

"Uh, we were at a friend's house and now were going home." Jonas' mind was racing.

"Home, huh. What's in the sacks?"

"Sacks?" For a brief moment, the brothers were thinking the same thing—*'drop the sacks and run,'* but they stood frozen in their tracks. Neither knew what to do. They just stood there looking guilty.

"Yes, sacks." The officer reached out, took Jacob's sack, and opened it. "Well, well, well, what have we here?" He pulled the six-pack of beer out and set it on the hood of the police car. Then he held out his hand for Jonas' sack. "Let's have yours too." He placed it next to the other six-pack before turning back to the brothers.

"I guess you know that this stuff is illegal for everyone and especially for you two."

They didn't answer.

"Do you know what the penalty is for having this?"

"No sir."

"Thirty days in jail and a fine...Are you boys sure you want it bad enough to risk the penalty?"

They stood silent and did not answer.

"Tell you what I'm going to do. You look like nice boys and I suspect that you've never done this before. I'd even be willing to bet that someone put you up to it, so I'm not going to arrest you this time. However, I do want to take you home and talk to your parents."

If it had been daylight, the officer would have been able to see the color drain from both their faces. The thought of going home and facing their mother was even worse than the thought of jail.

"Couldn't you just let us go this time with a warning? We promise we'll never do it again." Jonas pleaded.

"Our father is dead and our mother is not very well. This might be too much for her." Jacob tried to sound sincere.

"I'm sorry to hear about your dad, but I do have to tell your mother. I have found in my experience that mothers are tougher than we think. Now...where do you live?" The officer ushered the boys into the back of his squad car and closed the door. The heavy thud it made might as well have been that of a prison door. It's closing shut off any hope of escape and sealed their fates.

At home, Margaret had drifted off into a troubled sleep. She watched her beloved Will walking along the bank of the river, fishing pole in hand. He stopped, lay down the pole and began gathering wood for a fire. He started chopping the wood into smaller pieces. He stopped his work, looked at her, and smiled, just as he had in that other dream long ago. Yet, the sound of the chopping continued as the image of Will began to fade.

Margaret struggled to clear her mind and open her eyes. She knew the sound; it was someone knocking at her door.

She rolled over and switched on the light. The knock came again. Margaret pulled on her robe as she hurried to the door. Who could it be at this hour? Her hands felt clammy and there was cold sweat on her brow.

"Who is it?" She called.

"It's the police, ma'am."

The short reply was enough to cause Margaret's heart to race. Something must be terribly wrong for the police to come to her house in the middle of the night. She put her hand to her throat for an instance as a weak cry tried to escape. Her hands were shaking as she opened the door.

Whatever she had expected, it was not what she saw. Margaret was stunned. All her fear gave way to surprise and disbelief. Could those two boys standing next to the officer, with their heads down and eyes fixed on the floor, really be her sons? How could they be? Her sons were asleep in their beds.

"I'm sorry to wake you, but I caught these two boys with an illegal substance and...well...I hate to haul them off to jail. Sometimes talking with a parent works better."

Margaret looked from one lowered head to the other. "An illegal substance you said? What would that substance be?"

"Beer. Even if it were legal here, they are both under age."

"Did you say you have to take them to jail?" Margaret turned her attention back to the officer.

"Well, ma'am, I'm supposed to…but I hate to throw young boys in with some of that riffraff."

"Thank you Officer. You're very kind and thoughtful."

The two young offenders had not raised their eyes once during the entire exchange. They didn't dare. Of all the stupid things they had ever done, this was the dumbest.

"You boys get along now. I'm releasing you to your mother." The officer tipped his hat as he turned to leave. "Good night, ma'am."

Jacob and Jonas went silently to their room. Margaret absent-mindedly watched the police car drive away down the street. She didn't know what to do next.

In their room, the two brothers sat on their beds. Jacob whispered. "What do you think she'll do?"

"I don't know. She'll either scream at us or cry."

"Or lecture. Don't forget the lecture." They groaned in unison.

"I think I'd rather have her scream at me. It's easier to take."

"Yeah, I know." Jonas rushed to the door and listened. "Wait! I think I hear something." He pressed his ear hard against the door. "She's talking to someone."

"Do you think she called one of her friends at church?"

"Quiet! I can't hear." Jonas motioned to Jacob to be still.

He pressed his ear closer to the door straining to hear. He listened for a moment longer then abruptly left his post and returned to bed. He flopped down on his back and put his hands behind his head. He lay there staring at the ceiling in silence.

"What? What did you hear?" Jacob kicked the foot of the bed. "Jonas, what did you hear?"

Jonas answered without moving. "She was praying. If you want to know what she's saying, you listen. I'm going to sleep."

Jacob plopped back onto his pillow. "No thanks. I'm sure we'll hear about it tomorrow. The only thing worse than a lecture is a sermon."

Quiet settled in over the boys and Jacob was soon asleep. But Jonas found sleep harder to achieve. His mind kept replaying the words of his mother—the prayer she had intended only for God to hear. It had been the cry of a broken heart. Worry, grief, anger, sorrow...all these had been wrapped up in the tearful plea of the young widow and mother. Desperation, too, had found its way into her voice. Jonas didn't have to see her to know that she was on the floor kneeling beside their father's chest. She always knelt there.

Jonas had asked her once why she knelt beside their father's box to pray. Margaret had told him, "Because it makes me feel as though your father is praying with me—as though I'm not alone."

Jonas didn't want to think anymore. Thinking made him feel guilty. He rolled over and pressed his pillow hard against his ears trying to shut out the words in his brain. Eventually, he did find sleep, but it was a restless sleep filled with strange dreams and shadowy people.

Chapter 22

"There's got to be an easier way to make money." Jacob heaved a bale of hay onto the back of a pick-up truck. Jonas stood a few feet away wiping sweat off his forehead with a handkerchief. The hay field was littered with thousands of bales of hay. The square bundles tied with twine dotted the landscape in neat rows, and nowhere in the entire scene was a single tree for shade.

"Tell me again whose bright idea it was to get a job on a farm."

"This isn't what I had in mind." Jacob picked up another bale and threw it into the truck.

"Jacob, you have to stack them straight or they'll fall over."

"Why don't you stack them then." Now it was Jacob's turn to stop and wipe off the sweat streaming down his forehead and threatening to drip into his eyes.

"You know that's a good idea. You set them on the tail gate and I'll stack them." With that, Jonas hopped into the back of the truck and began straightening the bales of hay.

When the truck was finally full, the brothers flipped a coin to see who would drive the truck back to the barn. "I wonder how many trips back and forth to that barn we'll have to make?"

"I don't like to think about it." Jacob backed the truck up to the barn door and hopped out. "All I know is that we have a long way to go, and I don't ever want to do this again."

"What else could we do?" Jonas joined Jacob in removing the bales from the truck and adding them to the neat little rows already lining the barn floor.

"I don't know but there must be something." Jacob climbed up the stair step bales until he reached the top row. He picked his way across the mountain of hay until he reached the double doors that opened out onto the hot summer day. The blast of air that greeted him was a welcome relief. It felt almost cool compared to the stifling heat trapped inside the closed barn.

"What are you doing up there?"

"Resting."

Jonas made his way to the top of the barn and sat down in the open door opposite Jacob. They sat in silence for a time. With their backs against the doorframe, one leg stretched out in front, and the other bent with an arm dangling from the knee, they each looked like a reflection of the other. Together they surveyed the mountain of hay and watched the spiders building webs in the rafters. "It's hard to believe this barn is going to be full before we're finished."

"I know." Jacob mentally tried to calculate the number of bales already in the barn. "I wonder what happened to the guys who put these in here?"

"They developed brains to go with their muscles."

Jacob took off his gloves and looked at his sore hands. "I'm getting blisters. What about you?"

Jonas inspected his hands. "Yeah." He held them up for Jacob to see. "It's a good thing we're wearing gloves. Well, we better get back to work." He pulled his gloves back over his aching hands and began jumping from one bale to the next until he was on the ground.

Jacob was right behind him but stopped a couple of rows from the bottom. "Hand them to me and I'll start stacking a new row."

"Just remember to keep them straight and balanced."

"I know; I know."

They worked side by side hour after hour. They took turns driving into the field and back again. Time after time they loaded hay on the truck, drove back to the barn, and unloaded the hay. They repeated the same pattern over and over until at last the day was almost done. Never had the end of a day been so welcome to such tired bodies.

The brothers were covered from head to toe in sweat and dust. Every muscle in their arms and legs ached from lifting and climbing but their hands were the worst. The gloves had proved inadequate for the job. Somewhere in the late afternoon, Jacob had torn his handkerchief in half and wrapped the pieces around the palms of his hands then replaced his gloves. The extra padding helped, but the blisters, which had formed, had broken and had begun to bleed.

The work had become increasingly slower and more difficult. Their sweat mixed with the dust and dirt from the hay made them itch. The gloves became cumbersome and often hung-up in the twine on the bales; yet, they couldn't do without them. They began to use just their fingers for lifting, which soon caused them to be just as blistered and sore as their palms.

Finally, the day was over. As Jonas drove the last load of the day toward the barn, Jacob pulled off his gloves and winced in pain. "I don't think I can lift another bale."

"I know. Maybe we can unload tomorrow?"

Jacob groaned. "Tomorrow. I don't want to think about tomorrow."

"It'll be all right. We'll come better prepared." Jonas backed the truck into the barn and slowly eased himself to the ground. He was hurting just as much as Jacob. It had been a long day and both were exhausted. Jonas leaned against the side of the truck and carefully pulled off his gloves. He had followed his brother's lead and wrapped his palms with his torn handkerchief. They were bleeding also. He grimaced as he looked at his swollen and bloody hands. "We'll have to soak our hands in something and wrap them in bandages before tomorrow."

Jacob groaned again.

"Come on. Let's go home. I'm beat." Jonas draped his arm over the shoulder of his brother as they dragged themselves toward the barn door.

Once outside, they slid the two big doors into place and locked them with a board that dropped into a slot. In the distance, they could see a plump woman with gray hair standing on the porch of the farmhouse. She wiped her hands on her apron then held one hand up to shield her eyes from the sun's glare while placing the other on her hip.

"I suppose that's Mrs. Peabody."

"That would be my guess." Jonas began stuffing his gloves in his back pocket. The woman on the porch waved to them. The boys raised their tired and aching arms in a half-hearted attempt to return the greeting. They watched as Mrs. Peabody disappeared into the house.

"Now where do you suppose she went?"

"Who knows." They had reached the house by now and Jacob dropped down onto one step. "All I know is I'm tired and hungry and ready to go home."

"You boys have worked so hard all day I can't let you go without a snack." Mrs. Peabody had returned with two glasses of milk. "I've seen you coming and going all day. Hauling hay is such hard work." She held the glasses out to the boys. "I have sandwiches inside."

As Jonas reached for his drink, Mrs. Peabody's smile disappeared and a concerned frown took its place. "Look at your hands!" Jonas stopped and turned his free hand palm up. Mrs. Peabody took it in hers and examined it closely. Then she turned to Jacob. "Let me see yours. Is it just as bad?" Jacob nodded. "Oh, you poor dears! Come inside and wash them off good and I'll put some salve on them. They must hurt terribly."

The two exhausted boys followed Mrs. Peabody into the kitchen. They sat their glasses on the table and began to wash their hands as instructed. It was a painful task.

"Just when I thought they couldn't hurt any worse." Jacob twisted his face in pain. The soap stung, the water burned and every movement stretched and pulled the tender skin. "Jonas, I don't know if I can face doing this tomorrow."

"I know what you mean." Jonas was gingerly dabbing at his hands with a towel. "Boy, we thought we were so smart."

"What do you mean?"

"Mom. She tricked us."

Jacob thought about it for a minute. "She did didn't she."

"You bet she did. She knew how hard this would be. Instead of a switching or no supper, or even a lecture for getting caught with beer, she gives us days of back breaking labor and slow painful torture."

"And she lets us think it was our idea."

Jonas began to half smile. "Well, I guess it was our idea in a way. We did tell her we were learning to drive so we could get a job."

"Yeah, and a job on a farm. I guess we know now why she didn't scream at us about the beer. We should have known she wouldn't let it pass."

"Right. Two weeks of hard labor is what we got." Jonas smiled. He hated to admit it to anyone, but sometimes he envied his mother and her strength.

Jacob watched Jonas sitting at the table with a smile playing at the corners of his mouth. He began to smile too. "It was a good joke on us wasn't it." Jonas shook his head. "I guess we could take lessons from Mom in being clever."

"Maybe, or just in thinking before we act." Jonas downed the last of his milk just as Mrs. Peabody returned.

"Here we are. This will make those hands feel much better." She twisted the top off what looked like a can of shoe polish and the black gunk inside looked and smelled like tar. She used a Popsicle stick to scoop out the black goo and dabbed it on Jacob's upturned palm. Next, she wrapped his hand with a clean bandage. "Leave this on until you're finished working tomorrow evening. I'll change it for you before you go home. In a couple of days your hands will be callused then you'll be fine."

Jacob read the label on the can as Mrs. Peabody began the same procedures with Jonas. "This is horse salve and it's made from tar!"

Mrs. Peabody laughed. "Don't panic. I know it smells bad and it's intended for animals, but it works great on people, too. We're all God's creatures after all and a cut is a cut."

Mrs. Peabody finished wrapping Jonas' hands and snapped the lid back on the small tin can. Jonas opened and closed his hands a few times. "You know, I think they feel better already." The boys prepared to leave. "Thanks, Mrs. Peabody."

"It was nothing. Here." She offered them each a sandwich, "I know you're hungry. Have one for the road."

The brothers were only too happy to take the offered food. It was a long walk home. "We'll see you tomorrow. Bye and thanks again." Jonas smiled as he started out the door. Jacob waved and nodded his agreement as he took another bite of his sandwich. With renewed energy, the two Bystander brothers set out for home. Their long day of work was done.

Chapter 23

The cracked and bleeding hands of the Bystander brothers were soon callused and tough just as Mrs. Peabody had said they would be. The hay was stored in the barn, and summer was drawing to a close. Working on the farm had left little idle time for the brothers to spend with their friends. But once school began, they were together again almost everyday, and some of the old habits and problems returned. The shed behind Tom's house once again became their home away from home.

That shed had been the scene of many activities of which Margaret Bystander would not have approved. This fall afternoon of 1957 was no different. The gang sat on milk crates around a wooden box that served as a table. The entertainment was to be a game of poker. The conversation was work.

Jacob had been explaining in great detail the many trials and unpleasant aspects of hauling hay. He was now in the process of demonstrating the only advantage associated with the job. He flexed his muscles and bragged, "I bet I could whoop any one of you at arm wrestling."

All eyes instinctively turned to Nick. He was the largest of the group and towered over Jacob. Nick considered the challenge with a smirky grin and asked, "How much?"

"Eight bits."

"Okay, you're on."

With those few words, the boys around the wooden crate quickly shuffled their positions and gave the two contenders more room. Jacob and Nick took their positions; their elbows planted firmly on the makeshift table. They gripped their hands tightly and stared eyeball to eyeball as they waited for Willie to signal the start.

With the word "go," the muscles in both arms tightened and grew hard. Their knuckles turned white, and the veins in their necks bulged as they each strained to direct all their energy to the hands locked in silent combat.

For several minutes, neither arm moved. The gang watched in mixed anticipation. No one had ever held Nick at bay for this long. Then there was a very slight movement—so slight, it was barely perceptible. The smirk on Nick's face disappeared. The hard lines and set mouth of determination took its place.

Jacob's bright blue eyes held Nick in a glassy stare as unyielding as his grip on the big man's hand. He channeled all his mental energy as well as his physical energy into the arm locked in battle. Again, there was a breath of motion. Jonas stood behind Jacob, his expressionless face hiding the smile he felt inside.

Gradually, the clinched fists drew closer to the table...then—in one sudden thrust—it was over. Nick's arm was down, and Jacob had won. The room erupted into shouts of disbelief and admiration. Jonas slapped Jacob on the back with a hearty, "Way to go, brother!"

Nick reached into his pocket and pulled out a handful of change. He counted out the four quarters and dropped them into Jacob's waiting hand. "Here. You deserve it."

Jacob took the money with one hand and gave Nick a friendly pat on the shoulder with the other. "You're a tough one to beat, Nick, but, like I said, that job had more than one benefit. I just wish it wasn't so back breaking."

"And hot." Jonas chimed in.

"And dirty." Added Jacob.

"And itchy." Jonas pretended to scratch his neck and arms.

"Right, who could forget that."

The group of boys returned to their original seats around the table. Nick shuffled a deck of cards and began dealing them. "You know there are easier ways to make money."

"And that would be?" Jacob asked as he picked up his cards.

"My uncle has a small place down in Tahlequah and can always use another driver to make deliveries." Nick took a quick look at his hand. He picked up the remainder of the deck. "How many?"

Tom held up two fingers as he tossed two cards to the center of the table.

Rob was next. "Three."

"One" went to Jacob and "two" for Jonas.

"I'll keep these." Practically every eye looked at Willie. He either had a very good hand or was going to run a very good bluff.

Everyone studied their hand as they rearranged them. Everyone, that is, except Willie. He apparently felt no need to rearrange anything.

"Okay, who's in for two bits?" Nick tossed a quarter to the center.

"Not me." Pete tossed his cards on top of the other discards.

"I'm out." Jacob added his to the growing pile.

Jonas gave his cards a last look. "I'm staying." The eight bits that his brother had just won from Nick sat neatly stacked between the two brothers. Without a word passing between them, Jacob plucked a quarter from the top of the stack and dropped it into the pot.

Nick watched the two brothers closely over the top of his hand. "Is there anything you two don't share?"

"Nope." They answered at the same time.

Willie tossed a quarter to the middle. "Here's mine."

"Fold." Tom tossed in his hand and sat back to watch.

With a mind to win back some of what he had lost, Nick decided to raise the stakes. "I think I'll up the annie to four bits."

Practically before the coins hit the table, Jacob was dropping two more quarters into the growing pot.

Willie let the corner of his mouth curve just a bit before he caught himself. He tossed in two quarters plus a dime. "See you and raise ten."

Nick heaved a sigh of resignation. There was no point in throwing away all his money on the first hand. "I'm out." It was now apparent that the contest would be between Willie and Jonas.

All eyes shifted to Jonas. He didn't show any hint of worry or concern. His soft blue eyes betrayed nothing, not a thought, not a word. "I'll see your ten and call."

Willie leaned forward and spread his hand on the table. "Two pair...kings and queens."

The eager faces of the gang turned to Jonas. Had he been bluffing or did he have enough to beat Willie?

Jonas had turned his cards face down on the table when the bidding had started. Now he began to turn them over one at a time. First, a three appeared, then another three. Next, a ten followed by another ten—two pair, ten high, not good enough to beat Willie's hand. Finally, the last card—the on lookers could not help but lean forward in expectation of the outcome—another ten! "Full house."

A round of sighs escaped as everyone let loose the breath they had been holding. Jonas allowed a shadow of a smile to pass over his face as he watched Jacob claim the pot.

"I knew you weren't bluffing!" Jacob chuckled as he stacked the multiplied coins on the table between them.

"Like I was saying, my uncle can always use drivers; especially ones that can keep their heads under pressure." Nick began scooping the cards together. "Whose turn to deal?" He shuffled the deck a couple of times before looking around the table.

"Mine." Willie took the cards from Nick and shuffled them a few more times.

"Driving what..." Jonas collected the cards one at a time as Willie dealt them. "Another hay truck?"

"Not hardly. My uncle needs drivers to make deliveries."

"What kind of deliveries?" Jacob was considering how many cards he needed.

"Moonshine."

"Moonshine!" Jonas looked at Nick across the cardboard box. "Are you nuts. We got into enough trouble with two six-packs of beer."

"This isn't the same."

"You're right. It's worse!" Jacob held up three fingers, and Willie passed him three new cards.

"No, you don't understand. My uncle has a farm down in Tahlequah. He sells produce to families all over Tulsa. Some of them buy his moonshine, too. All he has to do is put a jar or two inside a bushel of potatoes or corn and drop it off." Nick studied his hand. "It's easy—give me two. I've been along several times and watched him do it." Nick picked up his new cards, thought them over carefully, and then tossed them aside. "It's a lot more profitable than this game that's for sure." Nick pulled a pack of cigarettes from his shirt pocket. "Sometimes he drives into Joplin and picks up a load of beer and whiskey to sell." He tore off the wrapper and tapped the pack against the side of his hand. Three cigarettes slid into view. He pulled one out and cradled it expertly between two fingers. He held the pack out to Jacob. "He was telling me the other day that he could make a lot more money if he could make more pickups and deliveries."

Jacob waved his hand at the cigarette. "Not now."

Willie laughed and reached for the offered tobacco. "The Chief only smokes a peace pipe didn't you know that, Nick." Six pair of eyes looked from Willie to Jacob. A sudden tension gripped the room as they waited to see what Jacob's reaction would be.

When Jacob did speak, it was with a calm but firm voice. "I smoke what I want, when I want, and, unlike little weasels like you, I don't need to poke fun at other people to make myself feel important."

The sneer on Willie's face faded and a cloud settled over him in its place. Nick, Tom, and Rob waited with taut nerves wondering what would happen next. Willie was mean and could be vicious in a fight, which was why he was the leader. On the other hand, Jacob was tough, and the summer's work had made him even stronger than before. Moreover, he wasn't afraid of Willie. Then there was Jonas. His face didn't betray the slightest trace of fear or concern. He apparently expected Jacob to win any fight that might take place.

Gradually, the corners of Willie's mouth turned up into a grin. He was no fool. He wanted to be the leader and part of being a leader was knowing how to get people to follow you, how to handle challenges, reading people. Willie knew his gang. Jacob didn't want to be the leader. Jacob was not a threat to his position, but he couldn't be pushed around either.

"Oh, I forgot. You don't like being called Chief. But can you blame me for forgetting when you're always wearing that buckskin vest? It's an open invitation you know." Willie had decided to laugh off the challenge.

The tension in the shed began to fade. Tom, who had been holding his breath without even realizing it, released a sigh. Rob relaxed his shoulders. And Nick, perched on the edge of his seat ready to jump out of the way should anything or anybody come flying across the room, settled back into a more comfortable position.

Jacob dropped his cards on top of Nick's discarded ones. "Deal me out. I've got better things to do." He rose and started for the door. He flung it open with such force that it hit the outside wall and bounced back with a bang.

Jonas waited until Jacob was outside before tossing in his own cards and following him. "A good memory is often the best hand to hold."

Nick caught him by the arm as he was passing. "Don't forget what I said about the job."

Jonas nodded his head and then hurried to catch up to Jacob. Once outside, Jonas saw his brother waiting for him. He was leaning against a tree, hands in his pockets, standing on one foot, and resting the other foot against the trunk of the tree. He was staring off into the distance thinking.

153

Jonas sat on the ground next to him and crossed his legs. He plucked a dandelion from the ground and appeared to study it intently while he waited on Jacob to speak first.

"Why do you suppose we put up with him?" Jacob looked down at Jonas.

"Loyalty."

"Loyalty? What do you mean by that?" Jacob sat on the ground next to his brother.

"He offered to be our friend when no one else did. Now we put up with him and his remarks because he is still willing to be our friend...loyalty."

Jacob chewed on the idea for a few seconds. "Well, loyalty or not, he calls me 'Chief' again, I'll deck him."

Jonas smiled. "Only if you beat me to it." They both began to laugh. "Come on brother. Let's go home."

Jonas jumped to his feet and offered his hand to his brother. Jacob grasped the out-stretched hand and gave it a tug, pulling Jonas to the ground. At the same time, Jacob scrambled to his feet and began running in the direction of home. He called out as he went racing down the street, "Last one home does the dishes!"

This was a game they had played many times before and came as no surprise. Jonas had tumbled to the ground, rolled over, and bounced back onto his feet in one smooth continuous movement. He set off toward home in a dead run, closing fast on his brother's heels.

Chapter 24

The two Bystander brothers stood idle, watching the ebb and flow of the students as they traveled down the hall. The school day was just beginning. Any minute now the rest of the gang would arrive and they would join the river of students going to class. Jonas half watched for Willie and the others, while he took notice of the girls as they filed past. Jacob only had eyes for the girls.

Occasionally, he would nudge Jonas in the side with his elbow and whisper, "Hey, check out that one! The one in the red sweater." Or; "Did you see the blond? I think she's new."

Jonas allowed his eyes to follow Jacob's lead but had little to say. Now and then he would smile and nod his agreement. However, mostly, he was content to let Jacob do the talking.

Presently, a pretty blond standing in front of a classroom door with her back to them caught Jacob's attention. He looked her over with a practiced eye. He nudged Jonas with his elbow. "Jonas, check it out. I don't think I've seen her before."

Jonas turned to look in the direction Jacob indicated. He could see the blond standing with two other girls they knew. She turned slightly, and he caught a glimpse of her profile. It wasn't much, but it was enough for him to recognize her. A slight twitch in one eye was his only reaction, and he quickly brought it under control.

"You're right. She's new."

"I think I'll mosey on over there and say hello." Jacob began straightening his shirt and whipped a comb out of his pocket to give his hair a quick touch-up. "It'll save her the trouble of trying to meet me."

Jonas coughed slightly to cover a laugh. With a straight face he said, "I don't know if that's such a good idea. She doesn't look like the type who goes for high school boys. She looks like a college man type to me."

"They're all college men types until they meet me. Watch, I'll show you." With that, Jacob sauntered across the hall and came up behind the pretty blond. He slipped his right arm around her shoulder and in his softest voice said, "Hello, doll."

The mouths of the two girls dropped open with shock and disbelief at such a bold maneuver. The pretty blond remained calm and turned a stern face to Jacob. Her voice was steady as she replied. "I'm not your doll. I'm Miss Thompson…the new English teacher."

Never had Jacob moved so fast. His arm literally flew off the shoulder of Miss Thompson as though it was a hot stove. His cocky grin vanished, and he stepped back apologizing. The two girls began to giggle and Jacob could see Jonas from the corner of his eye doubled over with laughter. He apologized again and made a hasty retreat. His face was hot with anger and embarrassment as he approached Jonas.

Jonas turned sideways and tapped himself on the left shoulder with his right hand. "Here, It's okay to punch me. It was worth it to see the look on your face." His eyes danced with laughter when he added, "I told you she was a college man type but you wouldn't listen."

Jacob hesitated while he remembered the conversation of a few minutes earlier. "You tricked me."

"You tricked yourself."

It was true. Jacob could see that. His own pride had allowed Jonas to play a joke on him. His anger melted away and he gave Jonas a shove. "Come on. We'll be late for class."

The two brothers moved out into the thinning crowd. In the distance, they could see Willie and the gang just coming in the door.

"Looks like they just got here."

"Probably."

"Don't mention that little incident back there, okay?"

"I wouldn't dream of it." Jonas grinned. "But...there's no guarantee that someone else won't."

Jacob thought of the two girls who had been standing with Miss Thompson and he groaned. It would be a miracle if they kept quiet. "Oh, well." He sighed. "I guess it doesn't really matter. It's not any worse than anything else we've done."

"Just tell everyone that you were pretending not to know who she was and they'll think you're cool."

Jacob smiled as he contemplated his story. "You're right. How many other guys in this school would be brave enough to make a pass at a teacher." The wheels in his head were turning now.

"Just don't get too big a head over it. Remember, that's what started the whole thing in the first place." Jonas cautioned.

"Don't worry big brother. I'll be cool."

By this time, they had caught up to their friends. Tom was in the middle of explaining something when they joined the little band.

"...perfect."

"What's perfect?" Jacob asked.

"We'll explain later, no time right now." Willie moved quickly toward the class across the hall. "We'll talk in gym later."

The boys broke up and hurried in different directions as the bell for first hour rang. Jacob and Jonas only had one class together and that was gym. The school had made it a point to put them in separate classes except for gym. They suspected it was because the teachers wanted it that way.

Gym was just before lunch, and the morning went fast. It was the best place to talk. There was always so much noise from everyone else talking that no one noticed them. The gang could get together and make plans without getting in trouble or attracting too much attention.

Today was an outside day. They would be running on the track around the football field. The coach was looking for members for the track team, so everyone was required to try out.

Jonas lined up on the starting line between Tom and Nick preparing to run the mile. He talked without turning his head. "Okay, so what's perfect?"

Tom kept his eyes straight ahead listening for the signal to start. He whispered. "Selling beer from the trunk of the car."

There wasn't time for more because the signal to go was given, and they were off and running.

Jacob watched from the sideline as the boys started the first turn. The mile required pacing oneself and planning for the last few yards. For long distance running, Jonas was better than his brother, whereas, Jacob was the one to beat in the fifty-yard dash.

Jonas held back a little in order to run alongside Tom. He kept his questions brief in order to save energy.

"Whose car?"

"Varies."

"When?"

"After school."

"Everyday?"

"No…days change."

Another boy was coming up behind them, so all conversation ended, and Jonas turned his attention to the race. He slowly began to pull away from Tom and the other team members. He crossed the finish line second and walked around for several minutes cooling off. Eventually, he collapsed on the grass beside Jacob.

"Not bad."

"I can do better."

"So why didn't you?" Jacob wanted to know.

Jonas wiped his hand across his sweaty brow, and then dried it on his gym shorts. "Because I lost my edge trying to talk to Tom."

"What did he say?"

Jonas dropped his voice to a whisper and looked casually around to see if anyone was near. "He says they're going to start selling beer from the back of a car after school."

"Wow—how?"

"I don't know. There wasn't time to say more. I guess we'll hear about it later after school."

"You realize of course that this could mean big bucks."

"You realize how much trouble we could get into?"

Jacob looked at the calluses on his hands. "I'll take my chances."

The coach was blowing his whistle. It was time to return to the locker room and get ready for lunch. Once inside, the voices of the 35 boys echoed and created a roar that was almost deafening. Yet, somehow, in the midst of all the noise, they managed to hear the bell ring, and they made a mad dash for the cafeteria.

Just as the brothers turned a corner, they spotted Nick with Rob talking to a very timid looking boy.

"Uh-oh. Looks like initiation time." Jacob said as he watched Nick and Rob slowly back the boy toward a locker.

"Yep. Sure does." Jonas gave a quick look around, checking for teachers. Seeing none, a mischievous grin spread over his face, and a twinkle lit up his soft blue eyes. He gave Jacob a quick nudge. "Come on. We haven't got to do one yet." A few more steps and they were next to Nick and Rob.

"Hey, fellahs." Jonas was the first to speak. "Were you planning on initiating a new freshman?"

Nick twisted up his lips into a smirk. "Sure was."

"How about letting us do this one?" Jacob suggested.

Nick looked at Rob then back at the two brothers. He shrugged his shoulders. "Sure, why not. There's plenty to go around." He stepped back and indicated with a wave of his hand that the freshman 'was all his.'

The poor timid boy just stood there with his eyes bulging and wishing he were somewhere…anywhere else. He wasn't sure what was about to happen, but he was sure he wouldn't like it.

Jacob stepped forward and with a ceremonious air took the books from the boy's hands and placed them on the floor. Jonas reached behind him and opened a locker door. The poor freshman looked a little bewildered until Jonas motioned to him to 'step inside.'

The boy looked from one brother to the other. "You...want me to get inside?" He asked.

Neither brother said a word. They just grinned and nodded their heads 'yes.'

"But it's too small." He whined.

Jacob took a step toward him, and the boy moved closer to the gaping hole of the locker. He looked beyond Jacob and saw Nick's glaring face and folded arms. Somehow, he instinctively knew that his fate at the hands of the two brothers was better than what it would be in the hands of that other boy. He resigned himself to the inevitable as he turned sideways and put first one foot and one shoulder into the locker. He ducked his head and pulled the rest of his body inside as best he could. The door slammed shut allowing only a sliver of light to peep through the vent in the door.

Nick slapped Jacob on the back. "Nice job. That's one notch on your belt." He stopped and thought about it a moment. "Or is it a half notch each since you share everything with Jonas?"

"Why don't you let us keep score since you have so much trouble with numbers." Jonas scoffed.

Nick didn't think it was funny, but Rob laughed.

Nick turned sharply to face Rob. "What are you laughing at?" He demanded.

Rob put his hands out and took a step back. "Hey, don't get mad at me. You're the one who stepped into it."

"Yeah, well, I didn't think it was funny."

"Forget about it, Nick. Let's go get something to eat."

A meek voice called from inside the locker. "Can I get out now?"

Nick banged a fist against the door and yelled, "Shut up! You stay in there until we let you out!"

The boy inside the locker became instantly quiet and the four members of the Wily Gang moved off down the hall toward the cafeteria.

Later that day, they heard that a teacher, who just happened to be walking down the hall, heard faint calls for help. Apparently, a freshman boy had been trapped in a locker. The story was that he had shut himself in the locker on a dare and then couldn't get out. The other students involved in the dare remained unnamed.

Chapter 25

Margaret was sitting at the desk in her room writing. Jacob stopped at the door and watched her for a moment. The house was very quiet and she didn't appear to know he was there. A sly grin began to creep across his face. Very slowly and softly, he started moving toward Margaret. He carefully avoided the boards in the floor that he knew from experience would creak. He drew closer and closer until he was standing right behind her. He leaned over and, with his lips only a few inches from her ear, whispered, "Mom."

Margaret screamed as she jumped straight up out of her chair, spun around, and swung at him. The first blow missed him because he knew what to expect. Years of experience had taught him and Jonas to be out of range when they scared their mother. She always came out swinging when startled. The second and third blows he ducked and dodged.

By the third swing, Margaret was laughing and playfully slapping at him. "Jacob! You stinker! Don't sneak up on me like that!"

"Sorry, Mom." Jacob said through his laughter. "I couldn't help myself. It was too good an opportunity to pass up."

Margaret took another slap at Jacob and this time he let her find her mark. Then he gave her a big hug. His tall muscular body made hers seem small and fragile.

Jacob looked over the top of his mother's head and saw Jonas leaning casually against the doorframe with his arms folded. His feet crossed at the ankles and a big grin covered his face. "Did you see?" He asked.

"I saw. You still haven't lost your touch."

"Well, when you've got it, you've got it."

Margaret wiggled loose from Jacob's tight grasp and gave him a playful shove toward the door. "And what do you have?"

"He has the knack for being sneaky. He can sneak up on anyone and get away with it. I, on the other hand..." Jonas shook his head and sighed, "Seem to give myself away. I have to settle for observing the fun rather than participating."

"Fun, huh. Well we'll see who has the last laugh. I think you two can buy me dinner." Margaret pushed both boys down the hall toward the living room. "I was thinking of taking you someplace special to celebrate your graduation, but now I think I'm the one who should be treated to dinner. After all, I think I'm the one who worked the hardest to make sure you graduated."

Jacob put his hands in the air. "Okay, Okay. I surrender. What do you say big brother?"

Jonas held up both his hands, too. "Count me in little brother. I'll get some money and meet you in the car." Jonas trotted back down the hall to their bedroom. Margaret collected her purse, and Jacob escorted her to the car still teasing and poking fun as he went.

Jonas grabbed his wallet from the table by his bed and stuffed it into his back pocket. On his way back down the hall, he paused at Margaret's door. The lamp was still on at her desk. He crossed the room quickly and bent over to switch it off. His eyes instinctively glanced at the letter his mother had been writing when interrupted. The words penned at the top of the paper caught his attention. His hands reacted almost on their own as if drawn by a magnet. The letter began *'My Dearest Will...'*

You would have been very proud of your boys today. They finally graduated high school. There have been times when I wasn't sure they would finish. I can't help believing that this day would never have come without the constant prayers of close friends joined with my own. There were so many obstacles to overcome.

It was hard for them to adjust to city life. They missed the hills of Seneca so very much. Life here was so different for them. Still, they did finish. They were so handsome in their caps and gowns. I couldn't keep from crying when I watched them walk across that stage and receive their diplomas.

I feel like a major hurdle has been crossed. I have done the best I knew to do. Only time will tell if it was enough. The future is open to them now and they can be anything they set their minds to.

I hope you don't mind, but I gave them each something from your chest as a graduation gift. It was hard for me to part with anything of yours, but I felt it was time. I know that they will be leaving me soon and I will have to turn loose of the most valuable possessions you left me, your sons. I won't be with them in the days ahead, but perhaps having something of yours to see and touch will help them remember everything I have tried to teach them.

I gave Jonas the buckskin vest. Jacob used to wear it all the time, but, for some reason, he stopped wearing it several years ago. Now Jonas wears it from time to time. Your gold pocket watch I gave to Jacob. He seems drawn to it. He opens it and reads it whenever he has the opportunity. I think it must serve as a reminder of everything you believed in and died for.

You would be so proud of them. They're such handsome boys; no, I can't call them that anymore. They're men now. Where did the time go? It seems like only yesterday they learned to walk, rode their first bicycle, and started first grade. Now they're finished.

I am so proud of them in spite of the mischief they've gotten into in recent years. They are good at heart and I have no doubt that the day will come when their outside will line up with their inside. They will discover God's destiny for their lives and follow it. Until that time arrives, I will pray for them every day and love them unconditionally. I'm not always happy with the things they do, but I'm always proud of them. They have been my life, my joy, my reason for living. How I wish you were here...

The letter stopped there. Perhaps Jacob had interrupted or perhaps the words that might have followed were too painful to write. Either way, it ended. Jonas put the letter back just the way he had found it. When would he ever learn. Sometimes it was best not to know what their mother was thinking. Knowing what she thought only made him feel guilty. If she knew everything they did, she probably wouldn't think they were sons to be proud of. She would certainly not approve of their working for Harry, Nick's uncle, if she knew what they really delivered and how they earned their money.

The honking of a horn shook Jonas from his thoughts and he hurried from the room. Later, after they returned home, he would talk to Jacob about the letter. Maybe it was time for them to make some changes in their lives.

Chapter 26

An occasional stubborn bush or solitary clump of grass pushed its way through the solid rock that formed ridges along the east side of the falls. Some of the ridges were six feet high; others were only a foot or so. They lay one upon the other in jagged rows slowly descending toward the waters edge. In some cases, natural stair steps made the passage from the road to the water easier. All along the way, there were little pools of water to be found—the remnants of recent rains or a reminder that sometimes the creek reached higher ground. Today, the water was running low. A dryer than normal July had made the water level fall. As Jacob and Jonas picked their way across the stony earth, the jutting stones became rounded—worn smooth by centuries of water rushing across their face.

The sound of the water as it rushed over the falls grew louder as they approached it. The cascading water pounded the rocks beneath their white foam without mercy. The waterfall wasn't very tall, only about ten feet; still, it was magnetic. The ceaseless flowing and churning of the water and the never ending roar combined to draw admirers from miles around.

The people came to bask in the sun. They warmed themselves on the rocks. They cooled themselves in the pool beneath the falls, or they just sat on a ledge and studied the cracks and crevices in the rocks wondering how many other feet had walked this same ground before them.

The Bystander brothers were no different on this July morning. They had arrived before sunrise. They had camped the night before in their teepee in Seneca. It still stood where they had left it five years earlier. It seemed like a lifetime ago; yet, it seemed like only yesterday. The charred remains of their old home marked the spot where they had been born and almost died.

That night so long ago had brought many changes to their lives. It had closed the door to their childhood and opened the door to manhood. As many times as they had tried to cross the threshold and go back, they had found they could not. Only the teepee remained now. It was their only link to those happy carefree times spent roaming the woods with Johnny. It stood as a silent monument to what had been but would never be again.

They had spent the night talking about the future. School was behind them. They were nineteen and able to make their own decisions. Part of them wanted to come home to Seneca and part of them said Seneca was no longer home. It was the past and not the future.

They had awakened before dawn and driven into Joplin. The falls had become one of their favorite spots. The constant rumble of the water rushing over the rocks could drown out every sound except the sound of crickets chirping. The solitude of the place helped the brothers to think.

Jonas found a niche in the side of a cliff that formed a natural chair. He sat with his feet propped on the ledge below him and leaned back until his head rested comfortably against the flat surface at the top of the ledge. His face, turned upward, allowed him to watch the dark sky gradually change from gray to bright blue as the sun came up over the horizon behind him.

Jacob had picked his way down to the waters edge, fishing pole in hand. He did his best thinking waiting for a fish to bite. Just a little way past the pool at the base of the falls, the creek narrowed before continuing its journey south. Right where it narrowed, trees had managed to grow from what looked like solid rock. Their roots were partially exposed and trailed off into the water in a web of twisting tangles. It was a perfect home for catfish and perch.

Jacob stationed himself a few feet away from the tree and lowered his hook into the water. He then settled back to wait and think.

About an hour passed before Jonas joined his brother at the edge of the pool. By this time, three catfish lay on the rocks next to him.

"I see you've got our breakfast."

"We can eat as soon as you build a fire."

Jonas grinned. "Some things never change. You catch them; I clean them."

"Don't forget who cooks them." Jacob gave his pole a sudden jerk and pulled out another catfish. "I think four is plenty. I'll find sticks to roast them on while you get the fire going."

Jonas began filling a dry hole in the rocks with twigs and a few dried leaves. "What do you say to a swim while the fish cook?"

"Sounds good to me."

The two brothers set about their tasks of preparing breakfast like a well-oiled machine. Each knew their task and executed it with precision. Soon the fire was ready and so were the fish. Jacob had cut four thin branches from a tree, stripped them of their bark and sharpened one end. He ran the sharp end of the stick through the mouth of the fish and out the open end where the tail had been. Suspended in this manner, each of the four fish hung just above the low burning fire.

"Now we're ready for a fast swim. Twenty minutes and breakfast will be ready." Jonas checked to make sure the flames weren't touching the fish before he made his way to the pool. Jacob was already testing the water.

"Whoa! That's cold!" He drew back his foot for a moment.

"The only way to do it is all at once." With that, Jonas jumped in feet first. The water wasn't deep so he tucked his feet up under himself in order to completely submerge. He came back up out of the water in a hurry. "Cold! Cold!"

Jacob stood on the bank and started laughing. "I told you it was cold, but nooo…, you thought it couldn't be '*that*' cold."

Jonas splashed water on Jacob. "Cold or not, I'm having my swim. You coming in or not?"

Jonas swam off toward the middle of the pool and deeper water while Jacob gritted his teeth and took the plunge. However, instead of popping back to the surface, he swam underwater until he was close to Jonas. When he was just within reach, he sprang out of the water and dunked him. A few seconds later, Jonas bobbed to the surface coughing and spitting. Jacob laughed at first but when he saw Jonas disappear beneath the water again, he stopped laughing. He dove into the cold and searched the darkness for his brother. Fortunately, it was a small pool and the current was not swift.

The few seconds it took Jacob to find Jonas and bring him to the surface might as well have been an eternity. Jacob's heart was pounding hard with fear. He pulled the gagging and half-conscious Jonas onto the rocks and watched helplessly as he choked and vomited water.

"Jonas! Oh my God! What have I done! Are you okay? Jonas! Say something!" Jacob knelt beside his brother waiting for an answer.

Presently, Jonas stopped heaving and coughing. He rolled over onto his back and blinked at the morning sky. The warmth of the sun warmed his wet body as the smell of smoke and fish filled his nostrils.

A little calmer now, Jacob asked again, "Jonas, say something."

Jonas rose up on one elbow then pushed himself to a sitting position. Jacob reached out to help him as he struggled to get to his feet. Once he was standing, Jonas steadied himself before he popped Jacob in the jaw with his right fist. It wasn't a very hard punch but it caught Jacob off guard and caused him to stumble backwards.

"Say something? I'll say something..." Jonas doubled over and coughed a couple more times, "don't ever do that again!"

Jacob reached for Jonas, putting his arm around him and helping him to the warmth of the fire. "I promise I'll never dunk you again..." a cloud of remorse had descended over Jacob's face "if you'll promise me not to drown." The memory of what had almost happened was heavy upon his shoulders.

Jonas studied his brother for a few seconds before a spark of mutual understanding appeared in his soft blue eyes. "Deal."

In one word, the whole incident was put to rest in the hearts and minds of both brothers. Forgiveness was asked for and given. The cloud between them was gone and they were ready to move on.

They sat with crossed legs devouring their breakfast of catfish. Carefully, they picked the white meat from the tiny bones while they discussed their plans.

"I've been thinking, Jacob. We need to get real jobs now that we're out of high school."

"What kind of jobs?"

"For starters, how about one that isn't going to get us into trouble. Maybe one in a factory; one that pays steady." Jonas tossed a few fish bones into the fire.

"So you think we should stop transporting moonshine for Harry?"

"That's exactly what I think. Now that liquor is legal to buy in Oklahoma, there's not as big a demand for the nasty stuff anyway."

"That's true; we haven't been making as many drops lately." Jacob paused to think over the idea as he pulled another catfish from the fire. "Where do you suggest we start looking? What city?"

"Well, I think we both know there's nothing around here; so, I guess we should look in Tulsa."

"Okay by me."

Silence settled over the brothers for a time as each remembered in his own way all the happy times they had spent in this little corner of the world—the happy days of their childhood. Unfortunately, they were no longer children, and it was time to lay aside what they could never have again. Tomorrow was what mattered now.

Jacob picked up the pocket watch that was lying on his crumpled T-shirt next to the fire. He pressed the button that opened the cover. The words inside were a constant reminder to him of how uncertain and final life could be. Mother had said that she gave him the watch instead of Jonas because he needed it. He hadn't questioned her meaning, but he had always wondered at it just the same.

"Are you anxious to get somewhere?"

Jacob shook his head. "No. I was just wondering what time it was." A long pause followed while Jacob tried to put his thoughts into words. "Jonas, do you realize that he was only four years older than we are right now when he died."

Jonas stretched out his long legs and leaned back against a rock. He thought about his brother's words. The near drowning must have rattled Jacob even more than it had scared him.

"Do you think he knew he would die young?"

"What a stupid question. No one ever thinks they will die young...unless they have a disease or something." Jonas kicked Jacob's foot with his own. "Put that away. We have better things to do with our day." Jonas hopped to his feet and started stirring the fading embers of their dying fire. He picked his way to the waters edge, dipped his T-shirt in the water and carried it dripping back to the smoldering embers. He held the dripping shirt over it and began to twist it until he had wrung out all the water possible. Tiny specks of ash flew into the air and the last of the dying fire hissed at him.

Jacob held the pocket watch tightly in his hand as he pulled his dry shirt on over his head. He would put it in the glove compartment of the car until his jeans were dry.

"Are you planning on wearing that wet shirt?"

"Nope." Jonas climbed up the rocky ridges to their parked car and tossed the wet shirt onto the hood. He reached inside and pulled out his father's leather vest. Where it had once sagged on the skinny shoulders and narrow chest of a boy, the vest now lent its mystic of strength to the broad shoulders and chest of a man.

Jonas grinned at Jacob. "This works much better for catching the eyes of pretty girls, and it won't be long before they will be here to work on their tans."

Chapter 27

July 4, 1964, Independence Day, was a time of celebration, bar-b-ques, picnics, and fireworks. Jacob and Jonas had been invited to join their mother at a church picnic to be followed by an evening of singing and fireworks, but they had decided on a day with the gang instead.

The six friends had loaded their cars with ice chests full of beer and food, and headed for their favorite spot in Missouri, The Falls. The place was sure to be packed with swimmers and sunbathers all day.

They were not disappointed. The six friends staked out their spot early in the day and watched the people come and go in shifts. Families were the first to appear, but they didn't stay long. Then came the sunbathers, the teenagers. They dipped in the cold water periodically to cool their toasted bodies before stretching out on the rocks again. The gang watched with interest from a distance. No point in getting involved with "jail bait." They were waiting for the over eighteen crowd to arrive then the fun would begin.

The sun had been very hot and the rocks burned the feet of anyone who dared to walk on them without shoes. It would be long after dark before they would cool. The Wily Gang had camped out in one of the few shady spots available and sat in relative comfort throughout the day.

It was a quiet day of uninterrupted waiting, watching, and drinking. No one bothered them or ventured a conversation. They had a reputation and were avoided by those who wished to stay out of trouble. Trouble and the Wily Gang traveled in the same circle.

Lillian Delaney

By 8:00 o'clock in the evening, almost all of the people had disappeared. Only a handful of die-hard swimmers remained. Soon, they were gone too. The six men from Tulsa sat around their small campfire washing down the last of the hot dogs and marshmallows with cold beer—a July 4 tradition for the group. Later they would have the "fireworks war." It too was a tradition.

For the last couple of years, they had faced off against a group of local boys at the Low Water Bridge. They would bombard each other with bottle rockets, firecrackers, cherry bombs, and Roman candles. Each year the stockpile of ammunition got larger, and the battle lasted longer. This year was no exception. The loser was the one who ran out of firepower first, and the winner was the group still standing when the smoke cleared. The prize was the bridge and exclusive rights to The Falls until the next year.

The sun was beginning to slip low across the top of the trees. Willie pulled a plastic sack out of a box sitting close to him and reached for what resembled a hand rolled cigarette. He lifted a burning stick from the fire and touched it to the end. He took a long drag on it and held his breath as he passed it to Nick. Each boy in his turn did the same. The joint made the round twice before Willie emptied the tobacco from the end of a cigarette, placed the stub inside, and twisted it closed again. He finished off the remainder of the joint and pulled another from the stash.

Jonas sat in this circle of friends with his legs crossed, long hair braided down his back, and wearing his buckskin vest. Jacob was beside him, a beaded headband holding his long hair from his eyes with a somewhat thin mustache and beard adding years to his young face.

"So, tell me..." Willie asked between drags on the joint and trying to hold his breath. "Do you like...working in a...warehouse?"

"It pays the bills." Jacob answered as he took his turn with the foul smelling weed.

"You two always do things the hard way." Nick shook his head and half chuckled. "The real...money...is in this...stuff." Nick indicated the smoldering substance, which he was holding out to Tom.

"Work a regular job if you want, but..." Willie pointed to the bag sitting at his side. "I'll make more money tonight in ten minutes than you make in a week."

Rob nodded his agreement. "Man, it's so easy...a little trip to...Mexico once in...awhile...cash in my pocket..." He patted his hip pocket. "No taxes...no fuss."

"I've been thinking of expanding...if you two decide you...want in...let me know." Willie put the sack away and leaned back on the rocks with his hands behind his head.

Silence settled over the circle of friends as they waited patiently for the sun to slide down behind the trees. Meanwhile, the Bystander brothers calculated mentally all the things that they could do with a little extra cash. They would have to keep their warehouse jobs of course. Mother would be on top of them with a million questions if they had money and no jobs. They were on their own, but they preferred to avoid her piercing scrutiny and inevitable sermon whenever possible—both of which were usually followed by a flood of tears from her and an ocean of guilt for them.

Perhaps they would take Willie up on his offer. They could explain away some extra money without too much difficulty. After all, their other ventures had paid well. The moonshine and bootleg whiskey they had delivered for Nick's uncle years ago and the beer they had sold from their car after school had both been very profitable enterprises.

The shadows had grown very long while the brothers thought on these things, and the sky had become the soft gray color it often is just before full darkness swallows the day. Jonas stirred the ashes of the dying fire. There was no need to add more wood. They would not be coming back today. The gang would spend the night in Seneca in the teepee of the Bystander brothers. That too had become a tradition.

Jacob pulled out his pocket watch and checked the hour. "It's almost nine. We better head over to the bridge."

"What's your hurry?" Willie wanted to know.

"It gives us an advantage to be there first."

Tom nodded his head in the direction of their parked car. "We have all the advantage we need in there."

"Don't put too much faith in fireworks alone." Jonas cautioned. "Strategy is just as important."

"Strategy and nerve." Jacob added.

"Strategy and nerve, huh?" Willie pulled himself up to a sitting position. "You two have plenty of nerve but leave the strategy to me."

There was a momentary pause while the brothers considered this remark. Although they had been members of the group for seven years, Willie had a way of pushing them right to the edge. He had drawn imaginary lines in the sand many times and dared them to "step over." Each time, the brothers had managed to go around the line and avoid an actual fistfight. They had ended each challenge in a draw. To say they remained friends would be an overstatement. They had never really been friends. The brothers were members of a group-a gang. Their bond was with the gang not individuals. The gang had given them acceptance when they had needed it. Unfortunately, it was their association with the gang that had locked them into that one circle of society.

"Are we going or not?" Jacob did not wait for, nor did he expect, an answer as he poured the water from his ice chest on what remained of the campfire.

Willie turned and snapped his fingers at Tom while nodding his head in the direction of the car.

Tom, quick to obey, followed Jacob's example and drained the water from the ice chest before loading it into the back of the parked car. Rob did the same, and in only a few minutes, everything was loaded and ready to go.

The Bystander brothers had their own chest safely tucked away in the trunk of their car and were pulling away as the other four members of the group piled into Nick's car. Once they were alone, Jonas turned to Jacob. "I think we need to teach him a lesson."

"Willie, you mean?"

"Who else." Jonas looked back over his shoulder at the headlights coming up behind them. "Listen, this is what we'll do." In the short mile and a half between The Falls and Low Water Bridge, Jonas outlined his plan to Jacob. He pulled the band from his braided hair and shook it loose. He pulled two cans of face paint from the glove compartment of the car. By the time they reached the bridge, Jonas had his war paint on and passed the black, red, and white paint to Jacob.

While Jacob smeared paint on his face, Jonas opened the trunk of the car and began stuffing firecrackers and cherry bombs into his pockets. A quiver filled with bottle rockets

179

hung across his back. He checked to make sure he could reach them with ease before he began sticking Roman candles in his belt.

Once Jacob was finished with his war paint, he began filling his pockets with firecrackers and his belt with Roman candles just as his brother had done. He had a pouch filled with cherry bombs, which he slung over his head and one arm. It rested within easy reach of his right hand. Both boys were now ready. They lit their punks with a cigarette lighter and were ready to go.

The rest of the gang had taken little notice of the brothers. They had been busy stuffing their own pockets. Each boy had loaded himself down with as much as possible. What they could not carry on them, they would leave in a box behind a tree close to the bridge.

Shadows of movement were seen on the other side of the bridge and pinpoints of light made by punks danced around like lightening bugs. It was time to go. Jacob and Jonas joined the circle of young men. Willie and the other guys only gave the brothers and their painted faces a passing grin. They had seen this side of them before. The Bystander brothers took the annual campaign very seriously.

Willie held his lighter to a handful of punks. Once they were lit, he passed them around. They began to move toward the bridge, Willie in front and the two brothers bringing up the rear. Jacob carried the box of fireworks. As he walked, he very carefully removed the fuses from about half the explosives.

The other four members of the group were already on the east edge of the bridge when Jacob deposited the box behind a tree. He and Jonas joined them just as the fun began.

The group from Tulsa was outnumbered in terms of people. The Joplin crowd numbered about ten. However, more people did not necessarily mean victory, as the rivals would soon discover. Instead, it often meant easy targets and getting in each other's way. The Wily Bunch had always succeeded in winning with just six men. There was no reason to think this year would be any different.

The West Side began with a barrage of firecrackers and then moved on to bottle rockets. The sky was ablaze with noise and streaks of light as the rockets would suddenly catch and soar off in all directions. They landed in the trees, the bushes, and the water. Some bounced off cars as well as bodies.

The East Side began much the same, moving from the tame firecrackers to the more destructive cherry bombs. The dreaded cherry bombs put the West Side on the run. A firecracker might injure a hand that held it too long, but a cherry bomb could blow it off. It was not surprising that they were outlawed in later years.

Their supply of cherry bombs gone, the East Side switched to bottle rockets again. The West Side moved back up onto the bridge and renewed their assault. Tom ran for reinforcements. Jonas nodded his head at Jacob. It was time for them to make their move. They each took two Roman candles and lit them. They charged past Willie and Nick and straight toward their opponent. They whooped and hollered as they went with their punks clasped tightly in their teeth and a blazing Roman candle in each hand. The startled opposition scattered like chickens before the spectacle and the rain of fire. Willie, Nick, Tom, and Rob watched in stunned silence. This tactic was wholly unexpected.

About half way across the bridge, the brothers stopped. They stood back-to-back, one facing east and one facing west, with balls of fire shooting from both hands. As soon as one candle was almost expired, Jonas dropped it and reached over his head for a bottle rocket. He lit it on the punk held in his teeth and threw it. He dropped the second Roman candle and lit another. Thus it went; his hands were never empty or idle. Jacob did much the same. He held a Roman candle in one hand and hurled cherry bombs from his pouch with the other.

Willie and the gang had recovered from their initial shock by the time Jonas began throwing bottle rockets at them. They grabbed more fireworks from the box and prepared to meet the new challenge. However, to their surprise, they discovered that most of their reserve had been sabotaged. They were defenseless.

It wasn't long before both the east and the west side conceded defeat at the hands of the Renegade brothers standing in the middle of the bridge. Jacob and Jonas raised their hands high into the air. Their left hands were clasped together, and in their right hands, they held a Roman candle still blazing. For miles along the river, the sound of their war whoops echoed as the Bystander brothers proclaimed their victory.

The Brothers had made their point and met Willie's "line in the sand" one more time. The four men waiting at the edge of the bridge shook their heads and laughed. Willie smirked his crooked little smirk while he puffed on a cigarette. Jonas met his stare head on. "Like we said, strategy and nerve are more important than numbers."

Willie took a last drag on his cigarette before dropping it to the ground and stepping on it. "Maybe next year we'll let you two do it by yourselves while we watch."

Jonas laughed and said, "Maybe."

Quiet returned to the river. The Joplin group collected their wounded and went home. The battle was over for this year. The unexpected attack of the Bystander brothers had been a first for the annual contest, and everyone hoped it would also be the last...and it was.

Chapter 28

The lobby was filled with excited people. They were milling about smiling, shaking hands, and hugging each other. It was graduation day. More than one parent could be seen wiping away tears of joy.

Ruth Lancing stood watching the happy scene as one tearful mother approached her. The woman took Ruth's extended hand in both of hers. Her words of gratitude warmed Ruth's heart.

"I can't thank you enough for being here for my daughter. I..." The woman's voice cracked and her lips quivered a little. "I don't know what...would have happened to her...if it hadn't been for you...thanks for helping her."

Ruth gave the woman a quick hug and murmured a few words of encouragement to her. As she did so, she raised her eyes ever so slightly and watched a scene across the room. A man with dark hair was standing behind a table loaded with pamphlets. He was speaking with other parents and shaking hands just as she had done. He smiled and shook his head as he listened politely to one couple, then with a barely perceptible movement, he raised his eyes to meet hers. His smile broadened and his eyes sparkled with mutual understanding. Then she knew. Deep down inside, Ruth knew that the man was her husband. He turned his eyes back to the couple standing before him while somewhere in the distance a bell rang. She watched the man with warm feelings pulsating through her body. The bell rang again.

Ruth fought her way through the fog of sleep as the dream faded into mist, and she fumbled in the darkness for the phone. "Hello?" Her voice was groggy. "Hello?" Still no answer. "Hello?" She asked a third time. Only the dial tone answered her. She hung up the phone and rolled back over in bed. Wide-awake, her thoughts turned to the dream. Something about it was…unsettling. It 'felt' different from anything she had ever experienced. She could see it all clear as day—feel the emotion. It was more like a memory than a dream.

Ruth threw off her covers before getting out of bed. She slid her feet into her slippers and made her way to the kitchen for a glass of milk. Maybe it would help her get back to sleep.

It was very dark outside and the city was peacefully sleeping unaware of anything unusual having happened. Inside, Ruth couldn't shake her sense of expectation. She curled up in her favorite rocker by the living room window. She stared up at the night sky filled with stars and a new moon as she cradled the glass in her hands. Her mind kept replaying the dream, and, each time, it seemed increasingly real to her as though it wasn't a dream at all.

Time slipped past. Ruth was still sitting in her rocker by the window when the first rays of morning began to light the eastern sky. Sleep had eluded her.

"Might as well get dressed and go to work. I'll never sleep now." Before long, Ruth had finished breakfast and all the other things that she needed to do before she was ready to leave. The short drive to the Jonesborro Street Church was uneventful. In fact, Ruth reached her destination without even remembering the drive. She drove by instinct and years of repetition.

Inside, Peter was already hard at work. Dear, sweet Peter. He had worked so faithfully for so many years—first with her parents and now with her. She couldn't manage without him. Volunteers came and went, and were unreliable, but Peter was as solid as a rock.

"Good morning, Peter." Ruth gave him a peck on the cheek as she hurried past on her way to the kitchen. She pulled a tray of salt and pepper shakers from a rack and began to set them on long tables. Next, she collected baskets filled with napkins and placed them on the tables.

Peter leaned against the doorframe and watched Ruth as she performed these simple daily routines. Her actions were mechanical, and her face told him that her thoughts were miles away. "You have a very somber look today. Is everything okay?"

"Hum, oh, I'm sorry, Peter. Were you asking me something?" Ruth had finished with the napkins and was pulling an apron from a drawer. She tied it around her waist.

"I was saying you seem to have something on your mind. Is there anything wrong—anything I can help with?" Peter pulled a folding chair from the nearest table and offered it to Ruth. He found a second chair for himself as Ruth sat down.

"Nothing's wrong really. It's just that..." Ruth hesitated. She wasn't sure how to explain what was on her mind. Should she tell him about the dream? What would he think? Would he laugh at her—think she was a silly female?

Peter leaned forward and patted Ruth's hand in the fatherly way he often did. "It's okay. Take your time."

"It's just that...I can't get it off my mind."

"Can't get what off your mind?"

Ruth looked at her hands. She was afraid to look at him. If he was going to laugh at her, she didn't want to see it in his face. "I had this dream." She hesitated. "Only it wasn't like a dream at all." Ruth glanced up at Peter to see what his reaction was so far. He wasn't smiling, so she continued. "It felt real. You know how dreams are usually disconnected and nonsensical. This one wasn't. It was more like...a scene from a movie. It was very clear and orderly. I understood what was going on even though it..." Here Ruth hesitated unsure of how to continue. "Even though there were people in it that I have never seen, and I was involved in something that I have never done."

Peter stroked his chin as he thought over what Ruth had just related. She hadn't told him any details. Why? "What's bothering you? What was in the dream?"

Ruth looked away again and felt her face grow warm. Why was she blushing? How silly—blushing over a dream! She was too tense to sit still. She bounced off her seat and started straightening chairs. "I feel so silly talking like this, but I can't help feeling that it was more than a dream. It was more like the future, Peter. I saw people I don't know; yet, I knew who they were." She couldn't quite bring herself to mention the dark-haired man. "How could I dream people so clearly I've never seen and know who they are unless God's telling me something? But what?" There...she had said it. She had finally put into words the thing that had been dancing around in her mind. She believed her dream to be a vision.

Peter had barely moved except to rest his hands on his knees. "So you think it wasn't just a dream, but that God gave you a 'vision' of the future? That's what's on your mind?"

Ruth had stopped and stood with her hands on the back of the chair she had occupied only a few moments before. "Yes, I believe it was a vision." She was much calmer now. Simply saying the words had lifted a weight from her shoulders. "Am I being stupid or naive? What do you think?" Her eyes and voice pleaded for an answer—a confirmation."

Peter replied with all the calmness of a sage. "An angel came to Mary in a dream and told her she was going to have a baby without knowing a man. Not only that, but the baby would be the long awaited Christ. Is your dream harder to believe than Mary's?"

Ruth couldn't keep from smiling. Laughter bubbled through her words. "Not hardly!"

"Mary believed the angel in her dream and hid the words in her heart. What about Joseph, Mary's husband—God spoke to him several times through dreams, and he obeyed what God said. He didn't question or doubt; he simply obeyed. Were you asked to do anything in your dream?"

"No. Not exactly."

"Then it seems simple enough to me. All you have to do is wait. Am I correct?"

Ruth wrapped her arms around Peter's neck and gave him a big hug. "You are so wise. Thanks for those words. I needed them."

Peter nudged Ruth toward the door. "I want you to go in your office right now and write down everything you can remember about your dream. Seal it in an envelope and put it somewhere where you won't lose it. Someday, if what you believe is true, and it comes to pass, you will want to read it." He gave Ruth another push. "Now go. I'll finish out here."

Ruth did as Peter commanded.

Chapter 29

It was November 1964; the summer had lingered longer than normal. The Wily Bunch, as they liked to call themselves, were planning another trip to the border. They would pick up a load of grass, party a little, and then head home. They had delivery stops all along the route from Brownsville to Tulsa, and their periodic drives south had become quite profitable.

It was a simple routine. Their contact would meet them on the military road between McAllen and Brownsville at a little place known as "Pete's" at a stop in the road called "Progresso." The exchange required three cars. Tom and Rob drove the point car past the meeting place and watched for the border patrol to approach from the west. The Bystander brothers drove the rear car and watched the east approach. Willie and Nick made the connection at Pete's. Each car had a walkie-talkie, which they used to warn the others at the first sign of trouble or the Border Patrol. The exchange had been made many times before without incident, but this time would be different. The transfer of goods and money had taken place as usual and all three cars were headed back to Brownsville when the point car began to sputter and choke ten miles outside of town. It chugged along for a few more miles and finally died. Tom called Willie on the walkie-talkie. "Willie…do you read me?"

"Go ahead, Tom."

"The car died. We can't get it started again."

"We'll pick up you and Rob; I'll wait for the rear."

"Gotcha."

Five minutes later, Rob and Tom climbed in the van with Nick and left Willie with the disabled car. As the van rolled away, the hair on the back of Willie's neck began to stand up. Something did not feel right, but he didn't know what. They were in the middle of nowhere. There were no other cars on the road. Empty fields stretched for miles leaving no place for a car to hide. Still...the uneasiness continued.

When the Bystanders stopped and Willie jumped in the car, he felt better but not reassured. "Did you guys see anything, anything at all that looked strange?"

Jacob looked over from the front seat. "Nothings stirring—no cars, no people, not even a jack rabbit."

"I know. It's too quiet. Hang back a little farther and when we get into town run the parallel route."

The brothers looked at each other for a few seconds then turned their eyes to the road ahead. Now they were nervous. Willie knew his business, and he thought there was going to be trouble. Willie was rarely wrong. He had a sixth sense about trouble. He was like a cat that always landed on its feet.

They entered town cautiously. The two cars traveled different streets two blocks apart. If everything went okay, they would meet at a predetermined spot and decide what to do about the abandoned car.

Suddenly, flashing red lights could be seen in the distance. Jonas turned off his headlights and crept up close to the scene. He stopped two blocks from the action, and Jacob got out of the car. Willie and Jonas waited while he ran through the alleys to see what was happening.

The van was sitting in the middle of an intersection completely surrounded and flooded in headlights. The lights from the police cars flashed red on all sides and the headlights seemed to come from everywhere at once blinding the men inside. Everyone was motionless…stunned by the surprise.

All at once, the dead silence was shattered as Nick screamed, "Scatter!" The men in the van threw open their doors and leaped out into the night. They began running in every direction as gunfire and shouts erupted in the darkness.

Rob was knocked to the ground within seconds of moving, tackled by three very large policemen. He never had a chance. They handcuffed him and dragged him to his feet then roughly threw him into the back of a police van. The other members of the gang were soon captured and joined Rob in the waiting van. The whole episode was over in a matter of minutes.

Jacob watched the officer who seemed to be in charge giving directions to the other policemen. He couldn't make out what the officer was saying but he could guess from the gestures that he was ordering a search of the surrounding area. Jacob backed down the alley staying well back in the shadows. Hopefully, he could get back to the waiting car and warn Jonas and Willie before the police discovered them.

He was too late. He came around the last corner just in time to see their car surrounded by police and Jonas laying face down on the hood of the car. On the other side was Willie.

Jacob shrank back into the darkness of the alley. He watched as Jonas, hands behind his back, and Willie were stuffed into a waiting car and driven away. He was close enough to hear the men beside the car talking.

"That makes five. Our information says there are six. Where's the other man?"

"Maybe he stayed with the point car?"

"Possibly. Send someone out to check on it. In the mean time, I want this whole area turned inside out. Those two weren't just sitting there for the fun of it. They were waiting for something or someone."

There was nothing Jacob could do here. He couldn't help Jonas by being caught. He ran as fast and as far as he could, making sure to stay out of sight as much as possible. He clung to the darkness in the alleys whenever he could. He paused periodically in dark doorways to catch his breath and listen for sirens.

He wasn't sure how far or in what direction he traveled, but the farther he ran the more silent and still the night became. When he finally ran out of breath, and his lungs were about to burst, Jacob ducked into an alley and huddled behind a stack of boxes. He rested there while he listened for footsteps or sirens, but the sound of his own heavy breathing was all he heard.

After a few minutes, his breathing became more relaxed, and he began to pick up the faint strands of music coming from somewhere near. He listened as the sound became louder and clearer. Someone must have opened a window and the night breeze carried the strands of the music and a heavenly voice through the darkness.

The words of the song were magnetic, and they aroused in Jacob a strange curiosity. He strained to hear them, but he was too far away. He inched along the alley hugging the rough brick in order to stay in the shadows. The police were probably still looking for him, and he didn't want to risk being seen.

The music grew louder...stopped...then began again. Now he could make out the words. Jacob stopped near an open window from which the light and music flowed. He sat motionless in the darkness and listened. A woman was singing—practicing a song. Now he knew where he was, the Church on Jonesborro Street. He knew the place. It was a small old building that dispensed food and shelter for the price of a sermon. Personally, he had never been hungry enough to need them, but he had known others who had visited there.

She began again.

"When doubt and disappointment hide the morning sun,
When all my dreams have ended, all my songs are sung,
His spirit soars within me, every doubt is gone,
I see a new horizon and sing a brand new song,"

Huddled in the alley, Jacob listened...The words vibrated through his bones. The fear and panic that had sent him racing through the back streets and alleys was beginning to give way to the realization of just where he really was and what he was really hiding from.

"When every road I travel leads back to where I've been,
When fears about tomorrow settle deep within,"

It was true. Every road he had traveled had only led him back to the same emptiness. Everything he had ever done had left him unsatisfied.

"He gives me new direction and takes the fear away,
He opens up the future and brings a brand new day,
For in his perfect timing,
Up ahead a light is shining,
And I know the dawn will be arriving very soon," (1)

The light from the open window seemed to grow brighter and the line between the darkness and the light became more distinct. A thousand little memories flooded his mind. He remembered all the times he had gone to church with his mother as a boy. He remembered the things he had heard and the things he had learned. Long forgotten words came pouring back into his thoughts as the words pierced his soul. It was as though God himself was speaking directly to him through the song. A voice, a sense of knowing came from somewhere deep inside Jacob telling him that these words at this time were for him and him alone. Jacob did not know how he knew, but he knew that if he didn't respond now he would not have another chance. This was his moment to step out of the darkness and into God's light.

Jacob unfolded himself from the dark shadows and stood up straight, and then he stepped out of the darkness and into the light of the open window.

---

(1)"He Opens a Window" by Ronna Jordan, @ 1982 New Branch Music (div. of C. A. Records, Inc.), Printed with permission.

Startled by the unexpected movement outside the window, the woman stopped singing abruptly. For a few seconds, their eyes met...then, as the woman prepared to run away Jacob spoke.

"Wait! Don't run! I was just listening to your singing...and I...I don't know how to explain it, but I need to talk with someone. Can I come in?"

The woman looked at Jacob, her body half turned with every muscle tense. She looked into his bright blue eyes and saw something in them that touched her heart. She knew he was telling the truth. She was no longer afraid. She motioned toward the front door with her head.

"The Church is closed now, but you can come in. Go to the front."

After Jacob disappeared from the window, the woman quickly opened a door near her and spoke to the man inside, "Peter, stay where you are and just listen in case I need you." With that hurried comment, she went to open the front door. Ruth Lansing was sure in her heart that she was safe, but she was no fool. Caution in this area of town and this time of night was wisdom. Years of experience had taught her many lessons in reading people. She had worked at this location and with the people who visited it for some time. Even as a child, her parents had taken her with them when they did volunteer work. She had seen many types of people throughout her life and was pretty good at spotting the fakes. She had also learned not to rely entirely upon her own judgment.

No...Ruth was no fool. She would talk with this man and see if he was sincere. She prayed a quick prayer. "God, I ask for your protection and guidance. Help me to discern the spirit of this man and to know how to help him."

Ruth opened the heavy oak door. The light across the street glared in her eyes and hid the face of the man before her. She stared at the silhouette in the doorway. He stood motionless with his hands at his side. Neither spoke. Finally, Jacob asked, "Can I come in?"

Recognizing the voice as that of the man in the window, Ruth stepped to one side and waived Jacob into the room. "Of course."

Once he stepped from the shadow of the doorway into the light of the mission, Ruth knew her instincts had been right. Something about the man sparked a note of recognition. She wasn't sure exactly what it was that made him seem familiar to her. She didn't know him; yet, she knew she could trust those bright blue eyes. She knew she had made the right decision.

Chapter 30

It was an hour or so later when Jacob left the Jonesborro Street Church. As he stepped out onto the silent street, he stood looking up at the stars—seeing them through new eyes. It had been many years since he had considered their creation or the one who had formed them and set them in space. The Great Creator of all life shown down from heaven and smiled at His new son.

Jacob closed his eyes and tried to take in all that had happened. It was almost too much for his mind to comprehend. Was it only this morning that he and Jonas had set out for Brownsville with Willie and the gang? It seemed like an eternity ago. How could he feel so different and still be the same person? How could he explain his transformation to Jonas?

Jonas—the smile faded from Jacob's face. What about Jonas? In his excitement and joy, Jacob had forgotten about his brother. What had happened to him? What was going to happen to him? Somehow, he needed to help Jonas. A mental picture of his brother surrounded by police flashed through his mind. He had to help him, but if he went to the police with questions, they would probably arrest him, too. He couldn't help Jonas that way.

Think…he must think. That's what he would do—find a place to stay and then think of what to do next. Jacob started walking down the sidewalk in the direction of a little place on Boca Chica Blvd. He knew they rented cottages or bungalows as they were called here. In his hand, he carried the small New Testament that Ruth had given him to read. She had told him to pray and read his Bible often. Jacob looked at the small Bible and warmed at the image of Ruth as she gave it to him. She had said it would be his guide in his new life.

Perhaps thinking wasn't what he needed to do after all. Perhaps what he really needed to do was read his Bible and let God tell him what to do. Jacob laughed at himself. He could hardly believe what he was thinking! Only a short time ago he was laughing at people who talked about God and the Bible. He had joined his friends in making jokes and mocking them. It was too funny for words! He had become one of THEM! At last, he understood everything his mother had been trying to teach him. Jacob's eyes grew moist as he thought of his mother. She had spent many years praying for her boys, and they had never given her dedication a second thought. He remembered her tears. He had considered them a sign of her disappointment; he realized now that they were tears of grief. She wanted them to know the joy and peace that she knew. She wanted her boys to know the security of an eternity in heaven. She didn't want to see them doomed to hell. Now Jacob understood why his mother cried.

In those few moments spent in prayer with Ruth, everything had suddenly become clear to him. He had a new understanding of how his mother could face the loss of her beloved husband, how she could raise two boys by herself, and how she could be content to face life alone. She had never really been alone at all.

Jacob suffered a sudden stab of guilt because he also understood how wrong he had been. He had treated his mother so badly and said so many ugly things to her in the past few years. She had always forgiven him, even when he didn't ask for it. His pride had insisted that he was never wrong, and he never needed forgiveness. How wrong he had been.

Jacob decided that the first thing he would do when he got settled was call his mother and tell her what had happened to him; then he would ask her to forgive him for all the pain he had caused her over the years. Last of all, he would ask her to pray with him about a way to help Jonas.

While Jacob had been thinking, he had covered the few blocks that brought him to his destination. It was the middle of the night, but there was still someone at the desk. After a few minutes, Jacob emerged from the office with keys in hand. Bungalow twenty-two was at the far end of a square of cottages that circled a courtyard.

The street was on the outside of the square and provided space for parking. On the inside of the square, a sidewalk traveled around a courtyard filled with palm trees, cacti, and sand. This would be a quiet place for Jacob to collect his thoughts and prepare to face the challenges of tomorrow, and tomorrow would be filled with challenges, of that Jacob was sure. But Jacob Bystander would not be facing the dawn alone; he would have God at his side and "with God, all things are possible."

Chapter 31

Bungalow twenty-two was small but Jacob didn't notice. He had everything he needed. He lay on the bed reading his Bible throughout the night. Every word was alive and new to him even though his mother had tried to teach him scriptures when he was small. Sometimes, while he was reading, he would come across a verse that he remembered her saying to him and Jonas when they were little. He wished he had listened to her more when he was a boy. Perhaps if he had…well the past could not be changed and wishing never accomplished anything.

Dawn would be arriving soon, and Jacob still didn't know what he was going to do to help his brother. He was also beginning to have doubts about calling his mother. He was torn between wanting to tell her about what had happened to him, and not wanting to tell her about Jonas. Maybe it would be better to wait until he had more information, and then call her.

Jacob had stretched out on the bed to read. The Bible lay open across his chest as he stared at the ceiling and considered what to do next. The whole situation was such a mess. Part of him wanted to embrace a new life, forget everything in the past, and walk away from yesterday, but another part of him new that it would not be that simple.

Yes, he could embrace a new life, but he could not forget the past, because Jonas was trapped in the past. Neither could he walk away from yesterday, because yesterday held Jonas. So what was he going to do?

Ruth had said, "*Prayer can move mountains.*" Well, this certainly seemed like a mountain to him. Jacob closed his eyes and began to pray.

"God, I'm not sure I have very much faith in my prayers, but I do have faith in You. I need help...or rather...Jonas needs help. He is in a jam and I don't know what to do to help him. Show me how to help him, God. Let me have a chance to tell him about You. Thank you, God...amen."

It wasn't a very long or eloquent prayer, but it was a sincere prayer. Jacob felt a flood of peace and comfort wash over him as he drifted off into a dreamless sleep.

When Jacob awoke, the sun was just beginning to top the trees outside his window. He quickly washed his face and brushed his hair before he started in the direction of Jonesborro Street. His desire to see Ruth was enhanced by the rumble in his stomach. He hadn't eaten since early the previous day.

Along the way, he stopped at a convenience store to buy a newspaper, a toothbrush, and tooth paste. When Jacob arrived at the Mission, there was a small crowd of transients gathering outside. The doors opened at 8:30 a.m. every day to the hungry. The meals were simple, but for the hungry, they were a feast.

Ruth had explained that the people were fed first and then they were asked to stay for a short service. She had said, "*It is easier to minister to those who are full than to those who are only thinking about their next meal.*" The services were never very long but designed to make as big an impact as possible in a short amount of time.

Well, if last night's song was any indication of the type of sermon or service that Ruth and Peter prepared each day, then Jacob had every confidence in their success. He smiled at the recollection of Peter. A short chubby man with white hair, Peter looked to be about as old as Moses. Apparently, he had been a very close friend of Ruth's parents. He had worked with them in various ministries and had continued to work with Ruth after her parents were killed.

While Jacob was thinking on these things, the doors opened and Peter ushered everyone into the Church. When his eyes caught sight of Jacob, he called.

"Jacob! Glad to see you! Come on in and join us!" He caught at Jacob's arm and pulled him aside.

"I thought I would stop by and maybe help…if you need me?"

"Of course! We're always happy to have extra hands to help out. It can get to be a big job running this place, and the workers are so few. We don't have the funds to pay people on a regular basis, and volunteers are so unreliable. It just so happens that today we are in great need of an extra pair of hands."

"Just tell me what to do."

Peter led the way to the dinning area. It was just a room, which had been added to the backside of the Church several years earlier. It had probably served as a classroom sometime in the past. Today, it held about six long tables surrounded by metal folding chairs. At one end of the room was the serving area. A couple of steam tables kept the food hot and another two tables held plates, dinner ware, and anything else that didn't have to be kept hot. All in all, the room seated about sixty people.

Jacob put on the apron handed to him by Peter and took a station behind the serving tables. On his left was Ruth and on his right was Peter. He looked at Ruth and smiled.

"Glad to see you came back to visit us." Ruth said warmly.

"I never thought I'd see the day I would be serving food in a soup kitchen and wearing an apron."

Ruth laughed. "Old things are passed away and all things have become new."

"You got that right!" They both laughed.

"Okay, cut the chatter; hungry people are waiting for their food." Peter was already pouring grits into bowls and placing them on trays as the people filed past. "Hi, Manuel…how are things going? Any word on a job yet?"

Peter talked and joked with the people as they came down the line. Once everyone was seated, he made the rounds getting acquainted with strangers and visiting with those he already knew. Ruth did the same thing. Between them, they managed to speak to everyone. Jacob fixed his own plate of food and sat in the kitchen alone. He watched and listened with keen interest.

After breakfast, Jacob stayed to help clean while Ruth and Peter held their meeting. By 10:00 a.m., all was quiet again. In a few hours, they would start the same routine all over again with the noon meal. Jacob promised to help.

He wasn't exactly sure why he was drawn to the place. Maybe it was the calm that he felt when he was there, or maybe it was the warmth extended to him by Ruth and Peter, or maybe it was because it was the place where he had finally met God. Whatever the reason, Jacob knew he had to come back.

He felt a twinge of guilt remembering that he still hadn't discussed Jonas with Ruth or Peter. The time had never seemed right to mention him. They hadn't asked why he was outside their window last night, and he wasn't sure he wanted to mention it either. Perhaps it was better not to bring up either subject just yet. He could ask around and find out what he needed to know on his own. Besides, he didn't want to get them or the church involved in his mess. No...It was better for them if they didn't know about the events that had brought him to their door.

Jacob looked at his watch; this was the quiet time of day at the gang's favorite cantina—the one they liked to visit on their trips through Brownsville. If he was lucky, he might find someone there who could give him the information that he needed. He would have to hurry. With only feet for transportation, traveling would be slow. It was a good thing that this was a small town.

Jacob said a hasty goodbye to Ruth and Peter with a promise to return in a couple of hours. He hurried out the door and down the street. Although he jogged part of the way, it still took him the better part of an hour to reach the cantina. The place looked deserted. Jacob tried the door; it opened into darkness. He had to wait for his eyes to adjust to the change in light before he could continue.

Finally, the old familiar hangout came into focus. There was the bar crowded with jars of pickled eggs, hot peppers, and sausages. Pictures of matadors in full costume and senioritas with flared skirts danced across the walls. Large ornate sombreros dotted the remainder of the stucco walls. Red tablecloths covered the small wooden tables while the wicker chairs sat bare of color. The place was empty except for the bartender and one customer at the bar. Both turned to look at Jacob as he stood just inside the door.

The man at the bar slid his stool back as he stood to his feet. The sound it made on the wooden floor was loud in the empty room. "Bystander? Is that you man?" There was a slight hesitation and a wrinkling of eyebrows before the man made up his mind. "It is you!"

Jacob met him in the middle of the room where they exchanged handshakes and punches. "Yeah, it's me. How you doin' Carlos?"

"Can't complain…staying busy…but what about you?" Carlos pulled out one of the wicker chairs and sat down at a table away from the attentive ears of the bartender. He dropped his voice a little lower. "I heard on the news this morning that your whole gang got busted last night and then I see you walkin' through the door!"

Jacob took the seat across from Carlos. "Did you hear any other news, Carlos?" Jacob motioned to the bartender. "I'd like a coke, please."

"What kind of news do you mean?"

"The kind they don't put in the newspaper." Jacob had had plenty of time to think while he was serving food and washing dishes. The events of the last couple of days had taken on a new light in the shadow of the police bust the previous night. Something was gnawing at Jacob and he wasn't sure what.

"Only rumors."

The bartender set a glass in front of Jacob and returned to polishing the bar and cleaning glasses with apparent disinterest.

"What kind of rumors?" Jacob sipped at his drink as he listened to Carlos.

"There is talk that the bust last night was a phony."

"That doesn't make sense. Why would the police pull a phony bust on us? What purpose would it serve?"

Carlos leaned closer and whispered. "Because, the bust was a DIA set-up. Evidently, the DIA has a mole in their office, and someone in your group made a deal with the FEDS to furnish them the identity in exchange for full immunity."

The gravity of what Carlos had just said struck Jacob like a fist.

"The Boss found out about the deal, but he doesn't know who the informant is." Carlos leaned back in his chair, struck a match, and held it to the end of a cigarette as he studied Jacob's face for signs of his reaction. Carlos leaned close once more as he lowered his voice even more so as not to be overheard. "Word on the street has it that—if not for the bust—somewhere between here and Dallas there would have been a very nasty accident." Carlos held up his hand and formed an "0" with his fingers. "A fatal accident. *No* survivors." He leaned back again in his chair, balancing it on two legs.

Jacob sat in silence as the full impact of what Carlos had said sank into his mind. It was clear to him now. Jonas had been unusually moody the last couple of weeks. He had intentionally picked several fights with his younger brother and then gone off on his own for a time. Jacob had never asked him where he had gone. He had assumed it had only been for a walk to cool off.

Jonas had tried to get him to stay behind on this trip. It was Jonas who had insisted that he get out of the car last night. If he had been in the car, he would be in jail right now.

Jacob picked his words carefully. "So you're telling me that the DIA pulled a phony bust in order to protect the informant?"

Carlos blew a ring of smoke toward the ceiling. "You know the Boss, he doesn't like loose ends."

"What happens now?"

"The arm of the organization is very long."

It was apparent from Carlos' words that he did not have much faith in the ability of the local police or the FEDS to protect anyone from the organization. "By the way," A note of sarcasm crept into his voice, and his eyes searched Jacob's face. "How did you manage to escape arrest?"

"By the grace of God, Carlos; I wasn't there when it happened." After a slight pause, "Carlos, I need to talk with Jonas. Do you know a way that I can do it without questions or being arrested?"

"Got any money?"

"Some."

"Sometimes—for the right price—the guards will temporarily become blind and deaf."

"Any particular guard?"

"I have heard that the midnight shift has very bad eye sight."

Jacob pushed his chair back and dropped some money on the table for the drink. "Thanks, Carlos. I'll be in touch. Keep your ears open will you. I'll be back tomorrow about this time."

Carlos blew another puff of cigarette smoke toward the ceiling as he watched Jacob leave the cantina. He was not as sure of tomorrow as his young friend.

Chapter 32

It was a pleasure to be around Ruth and Peter. They made doing dishes and cleaning floors almost fun. Jacob had never been as happy as when he was with them. One day at the Mission had opened his eyes to a whole new world—a world of devotion and service to others. It was quite a change for someone who had always been basically selfish.

Standing with his hands in dishwater, Jacob could hear Ruth singing in the little chapel. She had a beautiful voice and the words were piercing. He couldn't understand how anyone could listen to her night after night and not be changed. If only he could find a way for Jonas to hear her. What a difference she would make in his life, too.

Peter, Jacob had discovered, could preach a powerful message. He could say so much in just a few words. The things he said sounded just like the parables of Jesus. Would Jonas ever have the chance to meet them? Jacob's heart grew sad when he thought of his brother and the danger that he was in.

Carlos was right...the arm of the organization was long and its memory was even longer. If they found out who the informant was, they would kill him. Carlos had practically said that Jonas was the informant. He suspected it and if he did so would the Boss.

The dishes were finished and the singing stopped. Jacob sat on a stool listening to the sound of Peter's voice. He closed his eyes and let his mind wander back over his conversation with Carlos. He soon grew tired of thinking and tried to catch the words of Peter as they filtered through the door.

Eventually, Peter finished, and the people left. Ruth came to the kitchen to visit with Jacob. "You have been such a blessing to us."

"All I've done is a few dishes. You've done far more for me than I can ever repay." Jacob felt uncomfortable with praise or thanks. He never knew how to react—what was expected of him.

"There are many jobs that have to be done in a ministry such as this. Some are seen and some are not, but they are all necessary. There is more than one way to minister to people. Peter and I appreciate your helping today very much. You have ministered to us just by being here to lend a hand." Ruth's voice was sweet and floated across the room like the music she sang.

Ruth walked toward Jacob as she talked. When she was close enough, she reached out and brushed her fingertips along the edge of his beard. "I wonder what you would look like without the beard. It hides so much of your face, except for those beautiful blue eyes of yours."

Peter was passing the doorway at that moment and boomed from the other room. "And all that hair makes you look like a hoodlum!"

Everyone laughed, and Ruth took a step backward, flushed with embarrassment.

"I've had it since..." He started to say *'since he and Jonas had decided they wanted to look different,'* but they didn't know about Jonas. "I've had it so long that I don't remember what I look like without it." Jacob felt his beard with his hand as he considered what they had said. "I'm not sure I remember how to shave."

"It's like riding a bicycle; you never forget." Peter popped his head around the corner again and held up a razor. "In case you want to try?"

Jacob took the razor from Peter and put it in his pocket.

"You do whatever you want. It's your face." Ruth smiled back at Jacob and a nervous silence settled over them.

Jacob fidgeted a little then pulled his watch from his pocket. Should he try to talk with Jonas tonight he wondered?

"What a beautiful watch."

"It's a keepsake. I know it's old fashioned and big, but my mother gave it to me when I graduated high school. I guess she thought I needed it or I was old enough to appreciate it. I'm not really sure which."

"She must have been right on both accounts. You still have it."

Jacob put the watch back in his pocket. "Yeah, well, I guess I better be going. I'll come back tomorrow." Jacob held out his hand to Ruth.

The mounting awkwardness of their goodbye vanished into laughter as Peter's voice boomed once more from the other room.

"Don't forget the razor!"

"I'll take the razor..." Jacob dropped Ruth's hand as he turned to go. He paused at the door, turned his head, and shouted over his shoulder, "but I won't promise to use it!"

Chapter 33

There had been too much activity at the jail to risk a visit with Jonas. Jacob had watched at a distance for several hours before giving up and returning to his room. Maybe it was just as well. He had not worked out any definite plan yet, and, since he might only get one chance to speak to Jonas, it was better to wait.

Jacob went to the Mission the following morning and helped until after breakfast, just as he had done the previous day. The atmosphere there could almost make him forget for a few hours the burden he carried and the secret he concealed. When 10:00 a.m. came, he made his way back to the old familiar cantina.

He had been sitting in the Cantina for almost an hour waiting. He had taken the watch out of his pocket every ten minutes to check the time. He was growing impatient and worried. With growing anxiety, he opened the gold pocket watch one more time. A shadow fell across it, and Jacob looked up.

"Nice watch." Carlos pulled a chair out and flipped it around. He straddled the seat as he sat down and rested his arms on the back.

"It's about time. I have been waiting for over an hour. Do you have any news?"

"Sorry man. I got held-up."

"You got any more news?" Jacob repeated.

"Not much. The lid's on pretty tight." Carlos turned and barked at the bartender. "I'll take a beer over here." He looked back at Jacob. "What I did hear was that Jonas is in a cell by himself—separated from the other guys." Carlos watched Jacob's face intently. He could almost see the wheels turning in the young man's head. "Makes a person kind of wonder doesn't it."

The bartender set a beer down in front of Carlos, looked at them both suspiciously, and then walked away.

Carlos took a big gulp of his beer before continuing with that same sarcastic tone he had used the previous day. "I wouldn't want to be in Jonas' shoes right now."

Jacob had sat silent taking in all that Carlos had said. He hadn't wanted to believe it. He wanted to be wrong, but he knew that he wasn't. He cringed when he thought about the organization. They had the same information as he did, and it wouldn't be long before they put the pieces together.

"Thanks, Carlos. I have to be going. Later." Jacob left as quickly as he could. Time was running out, and he had to act fast if he was going to help Jonas.

Carlos watched Jacob fly out the door. He picked up his beer in one hand and swung his leg over the chair. In one sweeping motion, he spun the chair around into place. He preferred sitting at the bar when he drank alone.

Outside, Jacob needed time to think. His options were few. Carlos was right. The arm of the organization was long and their memory was even longer. Once they found out who the informant was—and they would find out—they would kill him. Even if Jonas got out of jail, he wouldn't be safe now. Nowhere was safe for him. They would make an example of him.

The hours that Jacob spent at the Mission that night were lost in a blur of mechanical routines. If he had been asked about it later, he would not have been able to recount a single person or specific moment. His mind was so preoccupied with thoughts of his brother and the terrible trouble they were both facing.

When he finally left the old building behind him, Jacob walked the streets trying to think what to do. Eventually, he was exhausted from thinking and returned to bungalow twenty-two. Once inside, his eyes fell on the open Bible lying on the bed. His hours of contemplation had convinced him of one thing—that in his own strength he could do nothing; only God could help them now. In His word, somewhere, there was an answer, and Jacob was going to find that answer.

He read far into the night until he finally dropped off to sleep. When the morning came, Jacob reached for the phone and began to call his mother. A few short rings later, she answered.

"Hello."

"Mom, it's me...Jacob."

The voice on the other end of the phone sounded relieved. "Where have you been? I've been trying to find you for two days. Is everything all right? Where is Jonas? Is he with you?"

The questions rolled out so fast that Jacob did not have time to answer. "Mom, slow down. Let me talk. We're in Brownsville. We had a little trouble, but everything's going to be okay."

"Trouble? What kind of trouble? You're not hurt are you?" She had expected this. Days before she had awakened from her sleep with a powerful urge to pray. An unreasonable sense of imminent danger had settled over her and would not leave. She had tried frantically since that time to find her boys.

214

"No, Mom, we're not hurt. I can't explain. I called because I knew you would be worried, and because I had something important that I wanted to tell you...You know how you were always trying to talk to me about God and about being saved? Well, I got saved a couple of days ago, and I just wanted to tell you." Silence. "Mom, are you there?"

On the other end of the phone, Margaret Bystander was crying. Her greatest desire in life was to see her boys serving God. Her greatest fear had been losing them forever. At last, she was seeing the fruit of her prayers. Her voice cracked with emotion when she spoke. "Yes, I'm here. You don't know how I have longed to hear you say that, or how much I have prayed for you."

"I'm sorry for all the years of grief that I have caused you and all the horrible things I've said and done in the past. I was such a fool. I didn't understand."

"You aren't perfect, but I love you. I only want the best for you." Her voice was shaky and charged with emotion. Jacob could see in his mind her quivering lips and watery eyes. He had seen them often over the years and repented for each tear that he had caused to fall from his mother's eyes.

"Thanks for all the years of sacrifice, Mom. Jonas doesn't understand yet, but he will. He'll come around, too; I'm sure of it. He just needs a little more time."

"I love you, Jacob. Tell Jonas that I love him."

"I will and I love you, too, Mom."

"Bye, Jacob."

"Bye, Mom."

It was hard to hang up the phone. There was so much more that he wanted to say to her, but there just wasn't time.

Jacob pulled the watch from his pocket and pushed the button that popped it open. He read the inscription that he had memorized many years before. Twenty-three. Their father had only been twenty-three years old when he died— so young.

Jacob closed the watch and returned it to his pocket. It was time to go. He paused on his way out the door to look at himself in the mirror. What would Ruth think of him without the beard and mustache he wondered? Perhaps he would make use of that razor after all. He needed a new look on the outside to match the new man on the inside. There would be time for that later. Right now, he had a date with a pretty girl and a feisty old man, and he didn't want to be late.

Chapter 34

"Still haven't used that razor I see." Peter grinned and stroked his own chin. "I feel a little bare. Maybe I should grow a beard, too."

"You tried to once—remember? It was pitiful." Ruth smiled playfully at Peter as she walked past him on her way to the kitchen.

"That's right, I did try it once." He made a face at Jacob. "The thing was itchy—drove me *CRAZY*!"

"Well, I've had mine since I got out of high school, but I'm getting a little tired of looking at it."

Jacob pulled an apron out of a drawer and threw it on over his head, wrapped the strings around his waist, and tied them in the front.

Ruth brushed past Jacob carrying a tray. Their eyes met briefly, but Ruth quickly lowered hers as she moved away. "Busy morning?"

"I called my mother to let her know where I am and how I'm doing. I didn't want her to worry."

Peter and Jacob were carrying large pans of food to the steam table, and Ruth was putting salt and pepper on the tables.

Ruth looked up from across the room. "You haven't mentioned your mother before. Does she live around here?"

"She lives in Oklahoma."

"Is that your home?" Ruth lowered her eyes and continued her work. She tried to make the question sound like idle conversation. Inwardly, she tensed at the possibility that Jacob was about to announce he would be leaving for good.

"Yes." The answer was short and final. Jacob did not like the direction the questions were going. He hadn't told them about his brother and wasn't sure if he should. Also, they didn't know about the trouble he was in. How could he tell them why he was in Brownsville or why he was outside their window? He didn't want to lie to them, so it was better to say nothing.

"Of course…we understand. This is not your home. You are only passing through." Ruth was disappointed. She enjoyed having Jacob around. Her face did not betray her thoughts and disappointment, but her voice did.

An uncomfortable silence hung over the three for a few moments.

"I don't know if I'll be able to help out tomorrow morning. I have something that I need to take care of."

Ruth and Peter exchanged glances. Each had avoided asking the questions that had played at the back of their minds since Jacob had first appeared outside the window.

"Of course…" Ruth hesitated. "You take care of whatever you need to. We'll manage…we always have. Right Peter?" Ruth was disappointed and she couldn't quite hide it from Peter no matter how well she tried. She enjoyed having Jacob around.

The cloud of gloom, which had settled over the couple, would never do. From the back of the room came the booming voice of Peter singing, "Got along without you before I met you, gonna get along without you now."

Ruth and Jacob both burst out laughing. The spell was broken.

"That's not exactly what I meant!"

Jacob rolled his eyes and shook his head from side to side.

"What a character! How do you put up with him?"

"Sometimes I wonder."

"Don't let her kid you, we make a great team, and she knows it. Besides..." Peter took Ruth in his arms, waltzed her around the room, and began to croon to her. "I light up your life...I give you hope to carry on..."

Ruth giggled. "That's you light up my life not I light up your life."

Peter turned to Jacob and held up both hands. "See I told you. She even admits it."

Ruth started pushing Peter towards the door while Jacob laughed even harder. "Enough! Go open the door!"

Order and sanity returned. The morning went as usual. Before long, everyone was gone, and the three found themselves alone again. They spoke very little; each one was lost in their own thoughts.

Peter wondered about the two young people who seemed to watch each other when they thought no one was looking. They were obviously interested in each other but neither would take the first step. He understood Ruth's reasons. She had come to the fork in the road once before. She had been forced to choose between God and a man she loved. She was not in a hurry to make that choice again.

Then there was Jacob—what about him? What could be his reason for caution? The possibilities were numerous, but most likely it had something to do with his visit to Brownsville and his mysterious appearance outside their window. Brownsville was a long way from Oklahoma. If Jacob was being cautious to protect Ruth, Peter was thankful. Time would reveal all.

Lillian Delaney

The day wore on and finally came to an end. Peter and Ruth said goodnight to Jacob and watched him disappear down the street. He didn't go straight to his bungalow. Instead, he made his way to the alley across from the jail and waited until it was quiet and only one officer was behind the counter.

Jacob had given a great deal of thought to what he was going to do. An idea had been planted in his mind, taken root, and grown into a plan. He could not make a mistake. Jonas' life might depend upon every word he said and every step he took.

The officer behind the counter did not appear very interested in what Jacob had to say. He looked with a blank expression at the floor, at the wall, even at his hands, but he never acted as if he heard or understood what Jacob was saying.

"I need to see Jonas Bystander. Is there a way I can see him...talk to him...even for only a few minutes? Do you understand?"

The officer only grunted. "Si, I understand. It is you that do not understand. I have said before no visitors. Now go away." He went back to looking at his hands.

Jacob was not ready to give up. He leaned closer to the man. "Is there a higher authority who could give me permission to speak to him?" Jacob turned his hand over so that the officer could see the money concealed underneath. The man didn't blink or twitch as he slid the money off the counter and into his pocket.

"There is a higher authority, but he is very busy and hard to reach."

Jacob reached in his pocket, pulled out more money, and slid it across the desk. "I am willing to wait until he is available."

The money again disappeared into the hungry man's pocket as he casually looked at his watch. "He comes in about this time every night, but he is only here for maybe ten minutes." He shrugged his shoulders and shook his head. "I don't know if he will want you to use up his few minutes?"

Jacob put more money on the counter. "I'll take my chances with the ten minutes." The deal now concluded, the officer motioned with his head for Jacob to follow him. They both walked down a narrow hallway to the cell where Jonas was.

The cell was small, dark, and dirty. Jonas was lying on a cot on one side of the room with his back to the door. He didn't move at the sound of the door being opened. No one spoke. The only sound was the clang of the cell door closing and the key turning in the lock.

Outside in the hallway the guard twisted his mouth into a sneer as he locked the cell door. *'Stupid man!'* He thought. *'I would have let him in for half the money he offered. Stupid...more money than brains.'*

The guard fingered the money in his pocket. He thought of all the ways in which he could spend it. He looked around as it suddenly occurred to him that if anyone knew of the bribe they might want a share—good, no one. All the money was his. With that happy thought, the guard returned to his station at the desk.

Once Jacob could hear the footsteps of the guard travel out of earshot, he spoke. "Jonas." His voice was loud in the stillness and Jonas jumped at the sound of it.

He was on his feet and across the cell in a few seconds. He grabbed his brother and gave him a big hug. "Jacob!" The smile faded as fast as it had appeared. "What are you doing here? I thought you got away?"

Jacob motioned to Jonas to be quiet. "I don't have time to explain. You must listen to me. I only have a few minutes. I am making arrangements to have you released. When the guard comes to let you out, don't talk to anyone. Go directly to that little place on Boca Chica Blvd. I have rented bungalow twenty-two. I'll leave the key above the door. Wait there. Someone will get in touch with you and tell you what to do next."

Jonas looked puzzled. "I don't understand? What's going on? Why are you acting so strange?"

Jacob looked over his shoulder at the locked door before he walked to the cot and sat down. "I don't have much time for explanations, so I have to make this short."

Jonas joined his brother on the cot.

"A lot of things have happened since I last saw you. I've been helping out at the Church on Jonesborro Street."

Jacob started to laugh.

"Just listen! I've been helping out there during the day. They are very good people. There's a girl named Ruth who runs the place. If something goes wrong, they will help you. I also had an interesting talk with Carlos. You're in great danger that's why I have to get you out of here quick."

"I still don't understand how you're going to get me out of here?" Jonas looked at Jacob with concern and doubt written all over his face.

"Trust me. I know what I'm doing." He put his arm across his brother's shoulders. "I haven't always been the smartest, and I know that you have had to bail me out a few times, but I have changed...in more ways than one." Jacob's voice had grown soft. "Jonas, do you remember all the times Mom tried to talk to us about God?"

"Of course I do...but I don't see..."

"Just listen! I understand what she was trying to tell us. I've changed Jacob, and when you're out of here, I pray that you will understand just how much."

Jonas got to his feet, walked a few steps away, and turned to stare at his brother. His forehead wrinkled with thought and his eyes studied Jacob intently. "Why are you acting so strange? It's as if you're a different person."

Jacob jumped to his feet, grabbed Jonas by the shoulders, and shook him. "Jonas! Listen to me! What I'm saying is very important! You *MUST* remember what I've told you! Will you remember?"

Jonas stared back into the eyes of his brother. "I'll remember."

Jacob gave his brother one last hug as he heard the sound of footsteps in the hall. "Remember...number twenty-two...Jonesborro Street...don't talk to anyone."

The key was turning in the lock as the brothers gave each other a final good-bye. Jonas watched Jacob leave through the open door, and then all was silent once again. He was alone with his thoughts. Questions about the strange way Jacob had behaved and talked whirled around in his mind. What could he have planned? How was he 'arranging' to have him released? Where was the rest of the gang? He hadn't seen them since the night they were arrested.

He took a deep breath and sighed. No point in losing sleep over what he couldn't change. Jacob would explain everything later.

Chapter 35

All morning Jacob had thought about what he was going to do. Time was all-important and time was running out. He had to tell Ruth about Jonas. There was no way to get around it. He would break it to her today before he left. He had also decided that it was time to part with the beard and mustache. They were part of the old life—the old Jacob.

While Peter and Ruth were busy with the afternoon service, Jacob went to work with the razor Peter had given him. He couldn't help smiling when he thought about what Ruth's reaction might be. Would she be pleased, disappointed, surprised?

When Jacob was finished, the face that stared back at him in the mirror was the face of his brother. It had been easy to forget that they were twins. The beard had made them so different that many of their newer friends didn't even know. They had wanted it that way.

When they were in high school, being twins was fun. They could play jokes on teachers, enemies, or friends. Once they were out of school, it just wasn't fun anymore. It was a pain, a nuisance. Looking alike caused all kinds of problems with girls and friends. So, on the flip of a coin, Jacob had been the one to grow a beard.

Jacob rubbed his bare chin. It had been a long time since he had shaved. He felt almost naked without all that hair on his face. Ruth thought he would look good without it, and Peter said he would look less like a hoodlum. Looking less like a hoodlum was very important to his plan.

Jacob heard voices approaching.

"Well, what do you think?"

Peter and Ruth stopped dead in their tracks, their eyes fixed on the stranger that stood before them.

"If I didn't recognize your voice, I'd swear you were someone else!" Ruth was wide-eyed with amazement.

Peter chuckled. "You don't look nearly as scary with that baby face!"

"What made you decide to shave it off?"

Jacob hesitated for a second before answering.

"It was time."

The two young people stood there looking at each other in awkward silence. Peter looked from one to the other before he said, "I think I'll go see what's cooking in the other room." He mumbled under his breath as he left. "Heaven knows there's plenty cooking in here."

Ruth blushed a little and Jacob grinned. They shuffled their feet and exchanged polite remarks for a moment or two until a serious look settled in over Jacob's face.

"Ruth...I have to talk to you." Jacob's tone was so serious that Ruth was overwhelmed with a sense of foreboding. She came a step closer. He continued. "I...I haven't been completely honest with you."

"In what way?" She sounded calm but inside her heart was racing.

Jacob hung his head as he hesitated. "The night I first came here I had been running from the police. I was hiding in the alley when I heard you singing. I wasn't just passing by." The silence grew loud as Jacob paused in his story. "I just didn't know how to tell you before, but now I have to."

"Why were the police after you?" Ruth tried not to let her imagination run wild.

"It's a long story so I won't bore you with details. It wasn't murder or anything heavy like that, but I was involved in something that was wrong. I was with some other guys and they were caught..." Jacob hesitated again and watched Ruth closely for her reaction. "My brother was one of them."

"Your brother?"

"My brother, Jonas. He's the reason I'm telling you about the trouble. I have to help him. I would give anything if I didn't have to tell you about my past, but I have to...for his sake."

"I see. And how do you plan on helping your brother?"

"I'm not sure. I only know I have to do whatever it takes to help him."

There was something in the way he said, *'whatever it takes'* that Ruth found disturbing. She could feel the panic mounting inside her as she watched Jacob begin to pace the floor. "Jacob, what are you suggesting? What are you planning to do?" Thoughts of smuggled weapons and a daring jailbreak flashed through her mind.

"I don't know what I'm suggesting. I only know that I have to do something fast." Carlos' twisted grin as he said *'the arm of the organization is very long'* flashed through his mind.

Jacob stopped pacing and stood in front of Ruth. He put his hands on her shoulders and looked her squarely in the eyes. "Don't you see? It is because I'm different that I must go." The urgency in Jacob's voice intensified as he spoke. "I must do everything within my power to give my brother the opportunity to know what I know, to experience everything I have experienced," His voice softened a little. "To have what I have. Do you understand?"

"Yes—I understand. I often feel the same desperation when I look out at the lost souls filling the pews day after day." Ruth slowly turned her gaze from Jacob's bright blue eyes to the empty dining room. "They come here looking for food for their bodies, when what they really need is food for their spirits—hope for the future." She turned to face Jacob. "I put my heart into my singing and pray that it will touch them and give them hope. Sometimes..." She reached out her hand and let her fingers trace the line of his clean-shaven jaw. "It does." Ruth began to mechanically fasten and unfasten the third button from the top of Jacob's shirt as she spoke. It was a nervous habit. "Yes, I understand why you must go. I will be praying for you and your brother until you return."

Jacob took both Ruth's hands in his and gently kissed her on the cheek. "Keep a pew warm for me?" He whispered in her ear.

Ruth smiled. "You know I will."

Jacob gave Ruth's fingers one last kiss as he backed toward the door and loosed his lingering hold on her hands.

Ruth stood firmly fixed, virtually glued to the floor, as she whispered her farewell. "Go with God Jacob Bystander."

There was a fleeting exchange of smiles between Ruth and Jacob...Then he was gone. Would they ever see each other again?

Ruth stood motionless staring at the door through which Jacob had passed. She could not shake the feeling of finality that gripped her. Nor could she understand how she could care so much for someone she had only known for four days. It did not make sense, but matters of the heart rarely did. She would have to pray and trust God with the future.

The voice of Peter calling from somewhere in the distance woke Ruth from her reflections. "Was that Jacob I saw leaving?"

Ruth shook herself and turned away from the door and back to the work at hand. "Yes."

"Where did he go? Is he coming back?" Peter looked from Ruth to the door and back again. His answer was written on her face.

"Perhaps I shouldn't ask, but what did he say?"

"It's all right, Peter. Jacob has to go help his brother; that's all."

"Brother? Where is his brother?"

"He's in jail."

Now Peter understood Ruth's concern. "I'm sorry Ruth. Is there anything we can do to help?"

Ruth let her eyes drift toward the window through which she had first seen Jacob. They lingered there for a few seconds, and then she looked at Peter's concerned face.

"You are such a good friend to me. Yes, you can help. Pray with me that Jacob's mission will be successful and for God's will to be done."

They joined hands and bowed their heads. Peter's simple prayer brought comfort and strength to Ruth. Peace settled over the room and both faithful servants went back to work.

Chapter 36

The sun crept over the treetops and the sleeping inhabitants of Brownsville. The only witness to the dawn's arrival was the eldest Bystander brother. He had not slept all night. The hard bed in the cheap little bungalow had offered little rest for his tortured mind. Another few hours would bring the news that he feared. His misery would then be complete.

He lay with his arm resting across his eyes. He wanted to hide the coming light of day. An unexpected knock on the door woke him from his troubled thoughts and fears. With great effort, he pulled himself from the bed and stumbled to the door. His trembling hand turned the knob and the door opened with a squeak of rusty hinges. The gloom that had blanketed his heart was tossed aside as he looked on the face of his brother. Joy rose from within him and spread across his face. Tears of happiness replaced those of sorrow as he embraced his brother. "I thought you were dead! How did you escape? I'm so glad to see you!" He released his grip and held his brother at arms length, then hugged him again.

"I can't stay. I only came to say goodbye."

"What do you mean? I don't understand." The smile quickly faded and his voice was laced with desperation. The arms, which had only a moment before embraced his brother, fell limp at his side, weighted down with guilt.

"I have fulfilled my destiny, and, because I have, I can leave you without regret. You are the strong one. You always have been. That's how I know you'll make it without me. You're destiny is yet to come. You have more work to

do—lives to touch—a world to change. My job is done; my time is finished. My destiny is fulfilled."

The words were final and the elder brother knew it. His heart wanted to argue, but the words would not come. "Then you are happy where you are?"

The smile that spread across the face of the younger brother radiated peace and joy. "Yes, I can go in peace knowing you will find your way without me. I have no regrets. Be what you're destined to be, and I'll see you again in the fullness of time."

The brothers embraced one last time. The younger brother turned and walked out the door as the elder brother watched in silence. He wanted to move, but he couldn't. He wanted to chase after his brother and stop him from going, but he couldn't. His feet were lead and refused to move. He stood frozen to the spot and watched helplessly as his brother turned, gave a last smile, and waved a final farewell.

The sudden slamming of a door shook the wall and startled the dozing man from his dreams. He rubbed his eyes and pulled at his hair. A dream...it had all been a dream. He was still alone in the empty little room. The waiting was unbearable. Perhaps the news was on. If not, at least the sound of the TV would break the dead silence. The little black and white TV set sprang to life.

"...the top story of the morning. In the local news, one of five men arrested in Friday night's drug bust was shot by guards in a failed escape attempt. Jonas Bystander was pronounced dead at the scene. Officers involved in the shooting were not injured. In other news..."

His brother dead? That's what the news had said—no—it couldn't be true! That's not the way it was supposed to be! That wasn't the plan! But it was true, and the truth of what had happened settled over the room. The TV continued to play but its voice went unheeded by the grief-stricken man. Sleeping neighbors woke up and started off to work. The day passed into evening and still the surviving Bystander brother wept bitter tears and mourned the loss of his brother. He could find no comfort for his aching heart.

The shadows became long; darkness filled the room and quiet returned to the streets once more. The neighbors were going to sleep unaware that inside bungalow twenty-two the tears had not yet subsided. Finally, drained and weak, the guilt-ridden brother fumbled for the switch to the table lamp.

The light from the lamp chased away the shadows in the tiny room but not those in his mind. It was a broken and hurting man that sat with his elbows on his knees and his face in his hands. He looked through his water soaked fingers at the small Bible that lay next to the lamp. His thoughts went back to that last conversation in the jail with his brother. In a sudden burst of anger, he picked up the Bible and threw it across the room.

It hit the wall and fell to the floor. It opened to a page that was marked with a folded piece of paper. The troubled and hurting man picked up the Bible and the paper. Again, remembering that last conversation in the prison, he opened the letter and read the words written there. As he read, the tears flowed even harder, blurring his vision. When he was finished, he began to read the underscored passages on the page, which the paper had marked.

And as Moses lifted up the serpent in the wilderness, even so must the Son of man be lifted up; That whosoever believeth in him should not perish, but have eternal life. For God so loved the world, that he gave his only begotten Son, that whosoever believeth in him should not perish, but have everlasting life. For God sent not his Son into the world to condemn the world; but that the world through him might be saved. He that believeth on him is not condemned; but he that believeth not is condemned already, because he hath not believed in the name of the only begotten Son of God.

(John 3:14-18)

He held the note in his trembling hands and read it again. The ink blurred and ran where his tears fell. The pain grew too great for him to bear alone. He stumbled out the door in search of the one person he could turn to in this lonely place.

Ruth listened to the news in disbelief as she was preparing to leave for work. Jonas was dead? What about Jacob? Where was he? What had happened to him? She recalled his parting words. He had been determined to help his brother. Had that help involved the failed escape attempt? If so, where was he? A thousand thoughts went through her mind as she switched from station to station looking for more information—nothing.

Eventually, Ruth had to leave. She could not ignore her duties at the mission. If Jacob needed her, he would look for her there. She must be there for him. She grabbed her purse and headed for the door. It was a short drive, so Ruth arrived in a few minutes…no sign of Jacob.

The day dragged by…Evening came and went…Still, there was no word from Jacob. The day was a blur of routine tasks and going through the motions of business as usual. Although she appeared calm on the outside, inside, Ruth was getting more and more nervous. Every hour that passed without word from him only served to increase her fears regarding his fate.

Finally, Peter couldn't stand it anymore. "Ruth, why don't you go home? He isn't coming."

"I have to be here if he needs me." She looked tired and worried.

"If he was willing and able don't you think he would have contacted you by now? It has been at least fifteen hours since the first news report."

"I know, I know, but I have to wait. You can go home, I'll be okay here."

"Not a chance. If you stay…I stay."

"Thanks, Peter." Ruth started to walk up and down the rows of pews checking for pieces of paper or other items left behind. She paused occasionally and let her eyes wander in the direction of the window—the window where she had first seen him. Each time she half expected to see Jacob there…he never was.

"You know those lights look terrible…think I'll clean them." Peter had been studying the ceiling lights for the last few minutes trying to think of something to say or do.

Now he virtually jumped from his perch on the piano bench and hurried to the back room for a ladder.

Shortly after Peter disappeared, Ruth heard the front door open. Normally, it was locked at this time of the night, but Ruth and Peter had been so preoccupied that they had not locked it. More startled than frightened, Ruth turned quickly toward the sound and caught her breath as she did.

"Jacob!" She called over her shoulder as she moved quickly between the pews and down the aisle toward the man at the door. "Peter, it's Jacob!" Ruth felt a rush of panic at the sight of him. He staggered into the room and crumpled just inside the door.

"Ruth?"

Ruth gazed down into the soft blue eyes, swollen and tortured with grief. "Jacob, we were so worried about you! We feared the worst."

"He's dead...My brother is dead." His eyes filled with tears as he sat numb looking at Ruth.

"I know; we heard the news report." Ruth could only guess at his pain as she struggled to find words to help...There were none. "Peter, get him a drink and bring me a damp cloth to wipe his face."

Peter hurried to the kitchen for the items Ruth requested.

The crushed and broken man sitting on the floor reached out and held onto Ruth's arm as he began to sob. "He's dead...and...and...it's my fault. I only thought to help him and instead I..." His words were interrupted by more sobs.

Ruth could think of nothing to say as the tears began to fill her eyes. She put her arms around him and tried to comfort him. She sat on the floor next to him and cradled him in her arms as she gently stroked his hair with her hand.

Peter returned with a glass of water and a damp cloth. "I think you better lie down. Let me help him to a pew, Ruth."

Ruth nodded her head in agreement. She relinquished her hold on him and quickly brushed the tears from her eyes. Peter helped Jacob to his feet and onto a pew. "Don't try to talk. Lie still and rest."

Ruth lifted her eyes to heaven and breathed a quick thank you to God for returning Jacob to her. She hadn't expected to feel this way, but she did. There was something about his heart that had drawn her to him. His eyes—those blue eyes—had pierced her heart in a way that she had not thought possible. Every time she had looked into them she had warmed all over and softened like butter in the sun. It was only now that she admitted to herself just how much she cared for him.

These thoughts were running through Ruth's mind as she held Jacob's hand and talked softly to him. The sound of her voice and the touch of her hand calmed him, and he grew quiet.

Peter, ever sensitive to Ruth's feelings, made an excuse to leave. "I have something to do in the kitchen. If you'll excuse me, I'll make myself scarce."

Ruth didn't look up. She nodded her head in agreement without taking her eyes off Jacob. Peter gave her a quick pat on the shoulder as he left them alone.

After he was gone, Ruth studied the face of the man lying motionless on the pew. His eyes were closed, and he was quiet. Dirt and whiskers covered the face twisted and pinched with pain. Ruth tenderly began to wipe away the grime with the damp cloth; the face of Jacob began to emerge.

With a sudden impulse, Ruth leaned over and kissed the unsuspecting man gently and tenderly on the lips. Instantly, his eyes opened and his hands instinctively reached for Ruth's arms. He held her at a distance. Their eyes met in a sustained embrace until Ruth drew back embarrassed and puzzled by what she had seen in his tortured blue eyes.

He was surprised. Why should Jacob be surprised? Had she imagined everything? Had she read more into his words and actions than he had meant? Had she misunderstood his meaning the day he had left to help his brother? Perhaps…or maybe it was just bad timing.

"I'm sorry…I shouldn't have done that." Ruth had turned away from Jacob in her confusion and embarrassment.

"No…I'm just…you caught me off guard…that's all." Jacob struggled to raise his hand to touch Ruth's hair. "I wasn't expecting such a warm welcome." He managed a tortured smile.

She held his hand and looked into the blue eyes that had always been able to melt her good senses. They seemed softer now than she had ever seen them before. Perhaps it was the light or sorrow that had dampened the fire, which had made them bright. But then again, maybe she just saw what she wanted to see.

At any rate, their moment was over. Peter returned and started barking commands. "Okay, times up. Ruth, you need to go home. Jacob can stay with me tonight and no arguments."

Ruth watched without seeing and moved without thinking as Peter gathered up Jacob. There were too many unanswered questions and too many new questions, which hadn't been asked yet. Ruth suddenly felt very tired. The weight of the last few hours had drained her of all strength. Her mind was too numb to think. There would be time enough tomorrow for answers. Tonight, she was satisfied to know Jacob was safe.

Chapter 37

Margaret Bystander had wondered at the phone call from her son. Something in his voice had sounded final—like goodbye. She tried to tell herself that she was being silly and reading into his words more than was there, but the uneasiness would not go away.

She prayed harder and more earnestly than before until, one day, she got another phone call which ended all her doubts. The police in Brownsville notified her of the death of her son, Jonas. Later a man named Peter had called to let her know where Jacob was staying. The police would not be releasing the body for several days, so she did not have to rush to get there. But Margaret had felt the need to be near her surviving son. When she arrived at the Jonesborro Street Church, Ruth and Peter greeted her. Jacob was out running an errand.

"It seems to help him to stay busy, so we find as much for him to do as we can." Peter explained.

Margaret studied the small chapel. "Jacob called me and told me of his new found faith." Her gaze came to rest on Ruth. "I think you must have had something to do with it?"

Ruth blushed. "I prayed with him, that's all."

"Why don't you tell her the whole story Ruth, I'm sure she would be interested." Peter urged.

"Yes, tell me the whole story." Margaret sat down as she prepared to listen. "I really would be very grateful for anything you can tell me about my son."

"There's not much to tell really. I was practicing a new song one night when I looked up and saw this man standing outside the window." Ruth indicated the window next to the stage. "I stopped singing...He asked if he could come inside...We talked for a bit, and then we prayed together." Ruth shrugged her shoulders. "That's all."

Margaret walked over to the window and looked out. There was a small alley that ran adjacent to the building, and on the other side was the Church cemetery. "You don't see many cemeteries next to the Church these days."

"I know. It's kind of spooky at night, but otherwise I like it there. I think I want my final resting-place to be close to the Church. It just seems closer to God somehow."

Their conversation was interrupted by the sound of the door opening. It was Jacob returning. When he saw his mother, he stopped in stunned silence. Neither Margaret nor her son spoke a word. They each seemed to be waiting for the other to begin. The waiting grew awkward.

Ruth and Peter exchanged glances. The unusual meeting puzzled them.

"Peter, I think that Mrs. Bystander and Jacob need to be alone. Why don't we find something to do?" They left mother and son alone.

When Ruth and Peter were gone, Margaret drew closer to her son. So close, that she could see the water in his eyes and guilt on his face.

"Do you want to explain...Jacob?"

He nodded.

"Let's take a walk outside. I saw a bench under a tree in the cemetery. We can talk there."

Mother and son sat on an old iron bench under a tall mesquite tree in the center of the cemetery.

Margaret looked around. "Ruth is right. It is calm and peaceful here."

"Mom, it's my fault…It's all my fault. He did it for me." His voice began to crack, his words were shaky, and the tears refused to be held back.

Margaret watched the birds flying from treetop to treetop oblivious of her aching heart.

"He wasn't killed trying to escape. He was murdered." Jacob took a crumpled piece of paper from his pocket and gave it to his mother. "Read this. It explains everything."

Margaret held the note in her trembling hands. She noticed the smudged places where the ink had run. As she read the words written there, her own tears rushed to meet those of her son.

"I see." She was too choked with emotion to say more. She folded the paper and handed it back to her son.

"Mom, the people who killed him are still out there. If they find out they killed the wrong man, they'll come looking for me."

Margaret thought over her son's words. She turned to face him. "Then you will change nothing? You are content to leave things as they are?"

"I will do whatever you want me to do." Jacob watched as his mother slowly rose from the bench. She walked forward a few steps then turned and passed a wise eye over the cemetery.

The cemetery was old. Some of the grave markers were hand made wooden crosses on which the names of loved ones had been carved. Family plots were marked off with iron railings, cement walls, or wooden railroad ties- whatever the family could afford. Cement crosses with lambs or angels on top dotted the landscape. In the middle of this solemn place, stood the giant mesquite tree. Its arms stretched out in a wide circle providing shade for all those who rested beneath it.

"I think that I want my son to be buried here—here in the shadow of the Church where he was given a second chance." She shifted her attention to her guilt-ridden son, looking him straight in the eyes. "And I think that you should stay here in Brownsville to help these people who have played such an important role in your life."

The eldest son nodded his agreement.

Chapter 38

The days and weeks that followed were long and painful for Ruth and Jacob. Both observed a silence and a distance, which was charged with electricity. Neither understood the actions of the other.

Jacob rarely spoke. He let his beard and mustache grow back. He moved about with an unseen burden on his shoulders that caused his eyes to avoid meeting those of Peter or Ruth. He appeared to go out of his way to avoid being alone with Ruth, although, she sometimes felt his eyes following her every movement. At other times, she would almost catch a glimpse of him standing just outside the door as she sang. It was only the slightest movement of a shadow that told her he was there listening.

Ruth knew Jacob was grieved by the death of his brother. Guilt was eating him up from inside, and she couldn't seem to reach him. She had tried a few times, but he had turned away from her. She regretted over and over again that one impulsive kiss. That one fatal kiss had apparently driven him away and, at the same time, drawn her even more under his spell.

The tension had grown increasingly worse during the weeks after Jonas' death as they waited for the body to be released for burial. When permission to bury Jonas was at last given, Jacob became even more withdrawn.

Jacob and his mother had decided to bury Jonas in the small cemetery next to the Church rather than transport him back to Oklahoma. The head stone read only "J. Bystander, died November, 1964." On Several occasions, Ruth happened upon Jacob standing at the window that looked out over the grave. Each time, he was staring at it with a far away look and pools of water in his soft blue eyes.

Finally, Ruth could stand it no more. She was determined to break through the wall that Jacob had built. Good or bad, she had to know what was in his heart. She could not bear the silence anymore. She could not bear watching him suffer alone.

Jacob had left bungalow twenty-two and had been staying with Peter ever since that fateful night. They came to the Church every day together. Jacob seemed content with that arrangement. When they arrived this day, Peter entered first with Jacob close behind. Ruth looked at Peter. The expression on his face and the shrug of his shoulders told her that nothing had changed.

Ruth handed Peter a list and said, "I have a few items that I need; could you pick them up for me?"

"Your wish is my command. Hold down the fort for me Jacob; I'll be back soon." Peter skated out the door before Jacob had a chance to respond, and the two young people found themselves alone for the first time in weeks.

Jacob moved across the room in a listless manner avoiding eye contact with Ruth and without comment. Ruth reached out her hand and caught him by the arm. "Jacob, wait. I thought we could talk for just a bit if that's okay with you?"

Finding himself forced to look at Ruth, Jacob tried to hide his thoughts and emotions behind a veil of indifference. "Talk about what?"

Ruth took a deep breath and motioned to him to sit down. She looked at him as he sat across from her. He was so handsome with those soft blue eyes and dark hair. All the other men she had known in her young life paled by comparison. Jacob was a genuine pearl in her opinion, and she treasured the time she spent with him even though they hadn't exchanged many words in the last few weeks. Being around him had brought her a mixture of agony and joy.

She had watched him when he wasn't looking—just as he watched her. She remembered the soft touch of his lips on hers. At other times, she would walk into a room where he had been and smell the lingering scent of the cologne he wore. In those moments, she would stand still and drink in the aroma while fighting to keep back the tears of longing to be near him. She wanted to share her heart with him, but was afraid that if she spoke too soon, he would reject her. The memory of his reaction to her kiss on that fateful night was still fresh in her mind.

Ruth felt awkward and stumbled over her words as she began. "Jacob...I sent Peter on an errand because I wanted to be alone with you for a little while...so we could talk." He waited patiently for her to continue. "I have been very concerned about you. You have been so quiet. You never talk about your brother. Sometimes it helps to talk about the loss of a loved one." Ruth paused to give him a chance to respond. He did not.

"I want you to know that Peter and I are here to listen if you want to talk. We...both of us...care about you very much. We want to help you if you'll let us."

Jacob didn't answer her. He pushed his chair back and moved toward the window overlooking the cemetery. He stood with his back to her. After a lingering silence he asked, "Why did you kiss me?"

Ruth was caught off guard by the question. "I...I don't know really." Her heart began to beat faster.

"Did I do something to encourage you? Did I make any promises?" His hands hung limp at his side as he continued to stare out the window.

"No...You didn't...not directly." Ruth could feel her face growing hot. "It was a combination of things I guess."

Jacob turned to face her. His soft blue eyes searched her face for clues to her heart. "What things?"

"Oh, things like shaving off your beard just so I could see what you looked like without it. The way you looked at me across the room. And...the kiss on the check." Ruth instinctively raised her hand and brushed it across her check before dropping her eyes to the floor. "The one you gave me just before..." Her voice trailed off leaving the sentence unfinished.

Ruth walked across the room and moved between Jacob and the window as though by doing so she could somehow keep the grave outside from coming between them. She stood with her back to him, afraid of what she might see in his eyes. "Did I read more into your actions than you intended?"

Jacob rested his hands upon her shoulders and gently pulled her close to him. He closed his eyes and allowed his lips to caress her hair. Ruth was sure that if he could not hear the pounding of her heart, he could surely feel it.

They stood motionless until Jacob whispered, "Ruth...I don't want Jonas to come between us anymore. You didn't misunderstand. I just wasn't sure if I had the right to feel the way I do. Can we begin all over again? As though we just met for the first time two weeks ago?"

A single tear ran down Ruth's cheek and fell to the floor. "But this one thing I do, forgetting those things which are behind, and reaching forth unto those things which are before."

Jacob turned Ruth around until she was facing him. Holding her in his arms, he lifted her chin with one hand. He looked longingly into her eyes and wiped the tear from her check…then gently kissed her on the lips.

In that brief moment when their eyes met, Ruth had the deep satisfaction of seeing the passion and tenderness in his soft blue eyes. For at least a few moments, the grief, anguish, and guilt that had clouded his heart had given way to joy.

Chapter 39

Ruth studied the notes on the paper in front of her. She had more time these days to practice her music and learn new songs. Since Jacob had decided to stay in Brownsville, things had really changed.

He had taken on a large part of the responsibilities of running the soup kitchen, which allowed Ruth and Peter more time for ministry. He had also been instrumental in getting funding so they could expand and hire help. Jacob was a blessing indeed. Ruth thanked God often for sending him down their alley and into the light of their window that November night more than a year ago.

She smiled as she thought of Jacob. He made her warm all over. Their relationship had improved dramatically after that December day when he had first kissed her and they had talked of starting over.

They were together almost all the time and shared a mutual devotion to God and His work. They talked sometimes of all the things they would like to do in the future. The soup kitchen was important, but there were so many other needs. Jacob did not want to be limited. He had great vision.

"Penny for your thoughts." Jacob had crept up behind her.

"Jacob!" Ruth instinctively swung at him. "Don't do that!" Jacob dodged her swing and grabbed her hand. He knew what her reaction would be. He had scared her before. "Missed me again!"

They both laughed.

Jacob sat down on the piano bench next to Ruth. His back was to the keys as he studied her. "Are you looking for a new song for Christmas or are you going to sing the traditional music?"

"I don't know. I can't decide." Ruth flipped a few pages of the book she had been looking through. "What do you think?"

"I think traditions become traditions because they satisfy the hearts and emotional needs of the people." He was gazing longingly at her, but she was busy with her book.

"That is such a profound statement that I am not quite sure what you just said."

Jacob looked up at the ceiling apparently thinking very hard. "Well, maybe I should put it another way. What are you doing New Year's Day?"

Ruth stopped turning pages and looked at Jacob with an air of exasperation in her voice. "What has that got to do with traditions or music?"

Jacob took Ruth's hands in his as he leaned forward slightly and spoke softly to her. "Would you like to observe an old tradition of changing your name on New Year's Day?"

He waited as Ruth sat in stunned disbelief.

"Well…Will you marry me?"

Ruth leaned forward and gave Jacob a soft kiss on the lips then threw her arms around his neck so hard he almost fell off the bench.

"I take it that is a yes?" He responded laughingly.

"Yes! Yes! Yes!"

The engagement came as no surprise to anyone. Peter and Margaret had both expected it for some time. It was agreed that the ceremony would be simple and take place on

New Years Day. The weeks passed quickly and soon it was Christmas Eve—only one more week until the wedding.

How Ruth loved Christmas! It had always been her favorite time of the year. However, this year it would take second place to New Years Day in her heart.

Ruth walked into the little chapel with a box of candles. It was dark outside, but the moon was shinning brightly through the window. It cast a long beam of light across the floor in the dark room. Ruth reached for the light switch but stopped when she saw a figure standing by the window. She stood frozen in sudden fear watching the man.

He turned a little, and, in the moonlight, Ruth recognized him.

"Jacob! You gave me a start!" Ruth breathed a sigh of relief. "What are you doing here in the dark?" She reached for the light switch again.

"Leave the lights off, Ruth." His voice had a sad note in it that stopped Ruth's hand in mid air and caused her heart to sink.

"Why, Jacob? What's wrong?" Ruth set the box of candles on the table by the door and joined Jacob at the window. She stood close to him as he put his arm around her.

"Ruth...I have to tell you something."

Ruth was scared. A knot tightened in her stomach and her heart began to beat faster with apprehension.

"I have to tell you something about me." He turned his face from the window and looked at her beautiful innocent face. "You may not want to marry me after I tell you."

Ruth's heart began to pound with fear as he continued.

"I...I'm not Jacob. I'm Jonas." He tilted his head in the direction of the cemetery. "Jacob is buried out there."

Ruth looked into those soft blue eyes that she had grown to love and adore. The fear that had threatened to overwhelm her melted away. "I know. I've known for a long time."

She watched as the corner of his mouth twitched and his eyes grew moist. "How?"

"I don't know exactly when it was that I knew, but I began to suspect what had happened..." She touched his lips with her fingertips. "When I first kissed you. You were so surprised. Jacob wouldn't have been surprised...and then there were your eyes."

"My eyes?"

"They're a soft blue. His were brighter."

"If you knew I wasn't Jacob, why did you let me continue?"

Ruth traced the line of his jaw with her index finger. "Jacob saw something in you worth dying for...I wanted to see it, too."

"And did you?"

Ruth held his chin in the palm of her hand as she spoke. "Yes...and much more."

That was all that he needed to hear. Jacob took Ruth in his arms and kissed her.

Chapter 40

I clicked off my recorder and sat down my pen. I was speechless, stunned by the revelation that I had just heard. Jacob was standing and looking out the window with his hands folded behind his back.

"One week later, Ruth and I were married." He turned back around and sat down at his desk. "What I have shared with you is important because of my reasons for sharing it." Jacob opened his desk drawer and held up a gold pocket watch.

"This watch is the reason I am sharing the story of Jacob and Jonas Bystander with the world."

I took the watch that was offered for my inspection. I opened it and read the inscription inside. I knew it was the watch belonging to Jacob, but I still didn't understand its importance.

"Perhaps I should continue with my story and its significance will become apparent."

A voice behind me interrupted. "May I join you?"

I turned and saw an attractive woman of about fifty-five.

"Miss Elizabeth, this is my wife, Ruth."

She smiled at me as she walked behind the desk and stood with her hands on her husband's shoulders. He reached up, took her hand in his, and gave it a tender kiss. "Now, where was I? Oh, yes. We were married on January 1, 1966."

"But if Ruth knew who you were, why didn't you change your name back?"

"At first I was afraid. Later, I came to realize that I really had died that day. Me...The man inside—the man I was." He closed his eyes as he struggled with emotion and searched for the words to express himself.

"My brother gave me a second chance to live so that I would have the opportunity to find what he had found…and I did."

He suddenly jumped up from his chair and walked to the window. He pointed in the direction of the cemetery. "The man that I was…died…and is buried in that grave along side my brother." He dropped his hands to his side then raised them again as he patted himself on the chest. "Everything that Jacob would have been, and everything that he would have done…has lived through me." His voice softened. "Jacob Bystander deserves all the credit for everything that I have done in the last thirty years. If not for his sacrifice, I would have been lost and nothing I have done would have come to pass. I wanted his name to have all the credit, which is why I let the name Jonas die with him. That is why I became my brother."

"Then why am I here? Why are you telling me this story? What does this watch have to do with it?"

Ruth replied. "Carlos knows that the watch belonged to Jacob Bystander. Carlos' cousin stole it from him after he was killed. Because Carlos knows the truth, he has threatened to tell the world unless we agree to help him. He wants us to laundry drug money, and that we will never do. He has threatened to destroy everything we have built. So, we decided that now was the time to tell the story ourselves. Once the world knows, he can't threaten us."

Jacob took Ruth's hand, held it to his lips, and kissed it again. "But that isn't the only reason. We think it's time that the world knows what my brother did. He made the ultimate sacrifice and he did it out of love." Jacob's eyes began to water. "I had a price on my head and he paid it. It should have been me, and it would have been, if not for him. It's time to share his sacrifice with the world. It's time for the world to know how great he really was. What he did thirty years ago was far greater than anything I have ever done."

He must have seen the question in my face, the doubt that filled my mind, because he pulled a faded and crumpled note from the desk and handed it to me.

"I know what I have told you today seems fantastic, but it is all true." He pointed to the note in my hand. "That is the note my brother left—the one I found in his Bible. Remember the dream I told you about? The one I had just before I met Ruth? I found the note after I had the dream."

I unfolded the paper carefully and began to read.

> *"Greater love hath no man than this, that a man lay down his life for his friend." (John 15:13) I do this one last thing because I love you and I want you to find the love, the peace, and the joy that I have found in these last few days. A part of me mourns the loss of tomorrow, but most of me accepts the destiny which has been appointed unto me. And I believe this is my destiny—to give my brother another chance at life. It seems I was destined to follow in the footsteps of my earthly father as well as my heavenly brother. My only regret is the pain I know you will suffer at my going, but in time, you will understand. You are the strong one, Jonas, that is how I know you can make it without me. Your destiny is yet to*

come. Embrace it just as I have embraced mine, and we will meet again.

My eyes were puddles and a great lump had risen in my throat, which prevented me from speaking. I refolded the letter and passed it back to Jacob. (I had not yet trained myself to call him Jonas.) He spared me the trouble of speaking.

"I believe God gave me the dream to comfort me. The words that my brother spoke to me in the dream were the same as the ones he had written in the letter. That knowledge gave me the faith and the strength to face what had happened and to go on with my life."

Jacob stopped talking. He turned in his swivel chair and sat with his hands folded looking out the window. The sun had set and the moon cast an eerie light across the tombstones in the old cemetery outside. I could see that his thoughts were walking that old path of years ago. Ruth stood close to him, watching his face, compassion clouding her own.

No one spoke. There didn't seem to be anything left to say. A blanket of solemn respect had settled over us, as each of us was lost in our own imaginations. I rose to leave. I expressed my gratitude for their time and politely excused myself with a promise to call the next day. My parting was acknowledged with a nod of the head and a wave of a hand, as I slipped quietly out the door.

I walked away overwhelmed with the enormity of what I had heard and faced with the awesome responsibility of telling their story to the world—and what a story it was! I didn't know if I could tell it the way it should be told. How could mere words convey such a history? Scribbled words on paper seemed so weak—so feeble. The depth of the love that had been displayed by Jacob was beyond my understanding. Yet, it was a real love that had given so much to the world, and to the lives of others, that I felt compelled to try.

I stopped outside the Church door and looked out across the street. Everything looked different to me than it had when I first entered that door. The street hadn't changed—I had. I could imagine that time thirty years ago when two brothers had started their day just as they had many other days. Yet, it had ended differently, and their lives had changed forever. They had traveled two different roads in time; one led to death and the other to life. Still, they had both achieved their destiny. Jacob had given his life for his brother. Jonas, in Jacob's name, had given his life to serving God and helping others. Together, the two Bystander brothers had reached out to and helped thousands upon thousands of people in the last thirty years. Could there be any greater fulfillment of God's destiny in one's life? I didn't think so.

I turned and looked again at the door of the Church, let my eyes drift up toward heaven for a moment then bowed my head. I took a deep breath and sighed. Maybe—just maybe—sharing this story with the world was my destiny? Perhaps it was the reason I was born?

I was suddenly filled with an overwhelming excitement! All my experience as a writer would be put to the test. Everything I had learned, had trained for, would help me to meet this challenge. This would be my greatest work. I knew in my heart that the story of the Bystander brothers would be the trumpet blast that would bring down the walls in many lives just as it had brought down the walls in my life.

The walls in my life that had held me captive to money and gain had crumbled. They had met their match in the unselfish devotion and love of the Bystanders. I walked away with a new sense of purpose and rejoicing in the knowledge that I would never be the same again.

About the Author

Lillian Delaney is a graduate of Northeastern State University in Tahlequah, Oklahoma and has called Tulsa home since 1979. She has a B.A. in Education and has taught English and History in addition to managing a C.P.A. firm.

A mother of four children, Lillian understands the struggles and challenges of single motherhood. She also knows the excitement that can be found in the unexpected as well as the planned events of life.

Her poignant stories are derived from her own experiences and a vivid imagination. She brings her own brand of emotion and depth to seemingly ordinary events, which allows the reader to become a participant in and not merely a reader of her books.

Printed in the United States
711800003B

9 781403 351876